NOT ALLOWED TO

LINDA MCBRIDE

AMBASSADOR INTERNATIONAL
GREENVILLE, SOUTH CAROLINA & BELFAST, NORTHERN IRELAND

www.ambassador-international.com

Not Allowed to Fail

© 2015 by Linda McBride
All Rights Reserved

This is a fictional work. Names, characters, places and incidents either are the product of the author's imagination or are used fictitiously. Any resemblance to actual persons, living or dead, events or locations is entirely coincidental.

ISBN: 978-1-62020-292-0
eISBN: 978-1-62020-397-2

Cover Design and Page Layout: Hannah Nichols
E-book Conversion: Anna Riebe Raats

AMBASSADOR INTERNATIONAL
Emerald House
427 Wade Hampton Blvd.
Greenville, SC 29609, USA
www.ambassador-international.com

AMBASSADOR BOOKS
The Mount
2 Woodstock Link
Belfast, BT6 8DD, Northern Ireland, UK
www.ambassadormedia.co.uk

The colophon is a trademark of Ambassador

DEDICATION

I would like to dedicate this book to my mom, Martha Ruth Tracy, who was my first editor and motivator. She passed away before seeing the finished copy.

To my oldest grandson, Kysen—how I long to see you again.

A special thanks to Barbara Higgins, who helped me polish my manuscript and showed me how much I had forgotten from my English classes.

CONTENTS

PROLOGUE

Charles Darwin held the manuscript close to his chest, protecting it as if it was an infant. Then he assessed the man to his left. The remainder of his life depended on his decision to publish his work, and whether or not he trusted his partner. He noticed the slow nod his friend gave and handed over the product: twenty years' worth of research, creative analysis, and his greatest idea.

It was the greatest idea of all time—of that he was sure. It was destined to shape the rest of his life and change the world. He felt pride in his accomplishment but worried about the controversy sure to follow.

"Charles," said his friend, "your father would be proud. You've come a long way since I first met you. Do you remember the last time we met in person?"

"It's not likely that I shall ever forget that meeting, Mr. Huxley," Charles replied with a laugh. "I think you called me a 'rambunctious hothead.' All I suggested was that you consider the facts and challenge accepted beliefs."

"I also overheard you mutter something about 'that pompous fool'; however, all is forgiven. The numerous letters I received from you eventually did persuade me. Now I believe that all the greatest minds agree with you. Most of them are in this room, and we're charting a path for your success."

Huxley took a sip of tea and put his cup on the table. He poured more of the strong brew from the carafe and smiled at Charles, motioning for him to have some.

"No thanks, Mr. Huxley. I'm too excited to consume any beverage at this time."

"Before I forget, there's someone I want you to meet," Huxley said as he looked around the room.

Charles felt a tap on his shoulder, turned around, and said, "Mr. Lyell, good to see you, sir. I owe so much to you and your books on geology."

"Save the accolades, my boy. I want you to meet a great believer in your theory. Charles, this is Ernst Haeckel, a prominent Prussian scientist. Ernst, Charles Darwin."

"Herr Darvin, it is such a pleasure to meet you," he said as he took Charles's hand in a pressure vise and shook aggressively. "I have brought some of my vork, vich I am sure you vill appreciate."

Charles winced and examined his hand for bruising while Haeckel looked for the item in his bag.

"Herr Darvin, I present to you proof of your theory. Observe these voodcuts. They are early-stage embryos that vill demonstrate the similarities between species as they develop."

Charles took the woodcuts. He marveled at the detail.

"Herr Darvin, on behalf of the Society of German Scientists, I congratulate you on your marvelous theory. Ve vish you great success and I, personally, vill do vhatever it takes to ensure your success. Vhatever it takes," Haeckel repeated.

He smiled, bowed respectfully, and walked away with Mr. Lyell. Mr. Huxley followed him.

Charles continued to stare at the drawings. There was indeed a resemblance between developing embryos.

What a fine day it is.

He looked out the window and noticed the unusually sunny day begin to darken as storm clouds approached. He felt a chill in the room and shivered. He looked for the closet where the coats were stored. As he turned to collect his coat, he felt a twinge of pain in his abdomen. He entered the large closet and found his coat.

Before he was able to put it on, a sharp, stabbing pain brought him to his knees. The pain was so intense he almost passed out. He felt nauseous with pressure in his ears followed by vertigo. He found it hard to breathe. The room appeared to be spinning.

He heard a shrill, buzzing sound. Then a light flashed. He thought it was lightning from the approaching storm, but the light became brighter, changing from a blinding white to blue, then green. He felt intense pressure, tingling throughout his body, and the nausea was unbearable. Everything faded to black—Charles fainted.

CHAPTER 1
FROGS

"Today we dissect frogs," the science teacher said as students entered the classroom and took their seats—half the class clapped; the other half groaned.

Gene ran down the hall and entered science class just as the bell rang. He dropped his backpack to the floor and slumped into his seat. He stared out the window, not caring to answer his friend, not caring if the teacher reprimanded him for being late again. He would have been happy if the teacher sent him to the office.

"Hey," said Carl in a low voice. "What's your problem today? You look like you had roadkill for breakfast."

Gene just shook his head. He was not calm enough to talk.

"Your dad again?"

Gene turned, gave Carl—who actually preferred being called C. M., short for Carl Mark—a sarcastic smile.

He muttered, "Bingo."

"He just wants the best for you."

"But I'm grounded this weekend. This weekend! We've got the tournament."

11

"Shh. We'll talk later. For now, just think about her," C. M. suggested and pointed to a brunette seated two seats ahead of them. "We pick lab partners today. You gonna ask her?"

Gene looked at her. Although he had yet to talk to her, he knew he was in love. She had the prettiest smile and wore outfits that looked strange on some other girls but very stylish on her.

He noticed her smile at a private thought and wondered what she had found so amusing. As he watched her, he felt the anger bottled up inside him ebb away. First, warm, fuzzy thoughts, and then he felt a smile fighting the muscles of his face. He cradled his face in his hands and dreamily watched her.

The smile gained only a momentary victory, as butterflies began to swirl in his gut; his anxiety level rose again. Talking to girls always made him nervous. He had yet to work up the nerve to say one word to her, and the semester was almost over. Since C. M. had challenged him, Gene was definitely going to speak to her. It was either that or be teased mercilessly at lunch.

She was smart. He needed all the help he could get to pass the class. Then his father might quit bugging him about his grades and that other *thing* they were supposed to discuss that evening.

Suddenly, someone pushed his arm out from under his chin, interrupting his daydreaming. At first, he thought he was in trouble for not paying attention. He looked up, expecting to see the teacher's angry look. Instead it was C. M.

"Look," he pointed at the kid next to him.

"Again?" Gene whispered and stifled a smile.

"Do it!" mouthed C. M. as he flicked his fingers.

He grinned and used his pencil to point to the kid next to Gene. Gene looked beside him and shook his head. Kaleb Jacobson had his science book propped in front of him for cover; he was fast asleep.

Some kids get away with everything.

He smiled mischievously, took a sheet of paper out of his notebook, and started folding it.

"Kaaa-leb," whispered Gene. "Kaaa-leb . . . it's time to wake up!"

Kaleb mumbled, "Leave me alone."

Gene looked at C. M., snickering as he insisted, "Go ahead . . . do it."

That was all the encouragement Gene needed. He looked down at the paper football with which he was toying. It had actually started out as a poem for Alexis, whose nearness two seats ahead of him had often prompted him to try poetry. Since he never seemed to think of the perfect words to write, the next best use for a blank sheet of paper was to fold it into one of his infamous footballs.

He positioned the mini-football on his desk and carefully aimed it at Kaleb's half-open mouth.

In a low voice, he narrated, "Here comes Gene Kysen, star extra-point kicker, for the crucial, game-winning field goal."

Then he snapped his fingers for a superbly arced kick. It sailed right into Kaleb's upper lip. His head popped up, and he glared at Gene and C. M., who tried to look innocent and not laugh out loud. Kaleb wiped the dribble off of his chin. "You just wait . . . I'm gonna get you back, but good!"

"Class is almost over, dude. It's lunch time," whispered Gene.

"Well, why didn't you say that sooner?" responded Kaleb as he yawned, stretched, and gathered his books.

"You're supposed to sleep at night, dude," said Gene.

"Oh? Really? No wonder I'm flunking science. You sleep at night and stay awake in the daytime. Got it," Kaleb responded with mock seriousness. "You should sign up for the rocket scientist career path when you fill out your classes for high school."

"Yeah? And you should be the monkey we send into space!"

"Do I get to sleep?"

"Sure, and you get paid for it too."

"Cool! I think I'm getting hungry for a banana."

"Good. Then let's get to lunch. That's enough problem-solving for the day."

"You'll make your relatives proud too," C. M. piped in.

"At least we no longer swing from tree to tree like your relatives still do!" Kaleb retorted.

"Hey, I resemble that remark!" said C. M.

"Uh-hum," interrupted Mr. Lyle, their science teacher, as he picked up the paper football from Kaleb's desk. "Speaking of careers and family trees, is your dad still on for Friday's Career Day assembly? He told me he was having problems at the lab."

"Far as I know," replied Gene with a shrug. "He's been kinda busy lately. We haven't talked much."

To himself he added, *Argued, yelled, or lectured is more like it.*

"Great!" Mr. Lyle said enthusiastically. "But that doesn't let you off the hook for your report. Ten pages, with citations on all the recent discoveries supporting evolution—or refuting it—if you can find them. With the project your dad is working on, I'm looking forward to what you have to say. You know, some people aren't too happy about the stance he's taking on the project."

"Yes, sir," groaned Gene.

He knew all about the problems his father was having at the lab. He heard about it every night. He should have plenty to write about, but he really did not want to do this report.

First, ten pages was an enormous amount of work he had not even started yet, although he had two months to work on it. Second, it was another area of friction between him and his father. He had learned creation in church and evolution in school. His father had a job offer with a Christian research project trying to debunk evolution. So his father constantly lectured him and tried to coax him into debating the issue. Gene did not want to argue about it. Third, he really did not care. He did not think it mattered much, anyway.

Who cares what I think?

"Oh, and as for this little matter," said Mr. Lyle as he held up the paper football.

Before he finished, a crackling voice came over the loudspeaker, "Mr. Lyle, can you come to the office?"

"Be right there," he said as he looked at the three students and then moved back to the front of the class. "Students, remember to read pages 152–165. Possible pop quiz. No problem for those who were awake and observing Mr. Froggie's little *surgery*. Jared, will you put Mr. Froggie back inside the cooler?"

There was no time left to finish the dissection, and Gene was disappointed. He had actually been looking forward to science class for once. He liked the idea of looking inside something to see how it worked.

After their teacher left the room, Jared, the JV quarterback, went to the front of the class and lifted the frog so everyone saw it.

"Now, class," he said, mocking Mr. Lyle, "our Mr. Froggie has had a rough surgery. It appears to me that we may have removed the wrong kidney, thus setting Mr. Froggie up for a nice lawsuit. But he croaked without any surviving relatives, so we lucked out on this one."

He snickered at his joke.

"Hey, I can't see from here," said Kaleb.

"You want a closer look? Here," said Jared as he tossed the frog to Kaleb.

The frog soared through the air, but not far enough. It landed on Avie Johnson's desk. At first, she just stared at it as if to consider who dared to intrude on the head JV cheerleader's space.

"Ooh! Yuck!" she screeched as she waved her hands as if trying to ward off something evil.

Then the kid next to her picked the frog up by its leg and tossed it at another girl. She screamed but was brave enough to pick it up and toss it in the air to get it off her desk.

It landed on Gene's desk. Everyone was laughing or screaming in disgust. Gene picked it up to examine it, but the odor of formaldehyde caused him to scrunch up his nose. With one hand he pinched his nostrils, and with the other he picked up the frog to toss it at Kaleb.

He looked at Alexis to see how she was reacting. She was squealing in disgust like the other girls. Gene laughed. That is, until he realized the frog had missed Kaleb's desk and landed on Alexis. Not on her desk, but on her!

There it was, straddled on top of her head. The look on her face was priceless. Gene started to laugh harder. Then Alexis's look of shock turned to disgust; she glared at Gene.

"Oh gross! Get this thing off of me before I croak!" Alexis yelled, unaware of her pun.

Gene meant to go get it, but he just sat there, horrified. She was not laughing, not at all. C. M. raced to her and clasped the frog between his fingers.

He held it up and joked, "Um, frog legs for lunch."

Then he tossed it across the room. Instead of landing on another desk, the dissected frog sailed out an open window. No one said a word. Several kids, including C. M. and Kaleb, jumped over chairs and desks to see where the frog had landed.

Sprawled out with its guts visible on a window of the art class, the specimen prompted more laughs as Kaleb shouted out where the frog had landed.

"Teacher's coming!" someone called out.

CHAPTER 2
ALEXIS

11:44 AM

Gene slammed his lunch tray on the cafeteria table, slunk into his chair, and moaned, "She'll never talk to me now!"

C. M. asked, "Who?"

"Lexy, oh, I mean, 'Alexis,'" mocked Kaleb.

"Oh, yeah," C. M. added with a laugh. "Too bad for you . . . She won't ever talk to you now. That was the evilest eye I ever saw!"

"I know!" Gene groaned.

Kaleb flicked his long bangs out of his eyes and said, "I'm sure Miss Perfect already has her science report done."

"It's about time to get your hair cut, ain't it?" C. M. asked.

"Heck no," answered Kaleb. "It's short enough in back to keep my old man happy and long enough to cover my eyes so I can sleep in class!"

"I wish my hair woulda covered my eyes so I hadn't seen that look in hers! She hates me. It's over before I even talk to her," moaned Gene. "And to think I was gonna ask her for help on my report."

"Hey, just be glad the bell rang when it did so we could get out of there," said Kaleb as he snatched one of Gene's french fries.

C. M. took a large bite out of his hamburger, wiped the ketchup off his chin with the back of his hand, and then wiped his hand on Gene's cargo pants. "Why not just ask your dad? He's a scientist, ain't he?"

17

"*Isn't* he, and, yes, he is! Here's a napkin to wipe your face off, jerk," Gene replied as he used another napkin to wipe off his pants. "You're lucky that doesn't show."

C. M. teased, "Waah . . . Crybaby!"

"So, you cool with your dad running the show tomorrow?" asked Kaleb as he yawned and flicked his brown hair out of his eyes again.

"Whatever," Gene responded as he nibbled at another french fry.

"Whatever? I'd love to have my dad be a respected scientist. Actually, I'd love to have a real dad. Not some drunk my mom had to kick out of the house," added C. M. It was usual for him to reveal his feelings about his father.

"Yeah, and I want to have the football coach pestering me to join the team 'cause I have the athletic build you do. And all the girls pestering me 'cause of my physique and curly blond hair! Besides, you don't have to live with him," mumbled Gene, eyeing the protein drink on his tray.

He did not have the appetite for it, but he did want to gain weight and add some muscle. He was thin—too thin—and always had been. He had just started a new protein diet and working out with weights. All he had to show for it were sore muscles he didn't even see!

Kaleb had the opposite problem: he was not thin enough. C. M. had neither problem. No matter what he ate, he had a good build. Even the wrestling coach begged him to join the team. All Gene wanted was some muscles to show off in time for summer . . . and to get his braces off . . . and to quit itching from that poison oak he got when his father made him clear out weeds by the garage. He rubbed a spot on his wrist that still had not healed.

"Well, maybe if you let your hair grow out, you can curl it too," teased Kaleb.

"Shut up!" Gene snapped. "My dad won't let me grow my hair any longer than this, but I do have a moustache starting."

"Let me get out my magnifying glass," C. M. taunted. "Yep. I see it. Hey, you know what will look good with that? A ring in your eyebrow, like mine. Got it done just last night."

"Yeah, I saw it," said Gene, "but my dad, letting me get that done . . . forget it!"

"Hey, no girl will be able to resist you—at least in your dreams!"

"I'm already being punished for something, and I don't even know what I did! He won't even let me go to game night anymore."

"But you gotta make it to game night this week! I know how we can get ahold of Alexis."

Before Gene could think of a good response, a loud voice interrupted their conversation.

"Hey, Carl!" someone shouted from across the cafeteria.

Gene turned toward the familiar voice of his sister, Sophie.

"Oh brother," he muttered. "The day has gone from bad to worse."

"Hey, Carl!" Kaleb mocked the high pitch of Sophie's voice and leaned over to Gene. "It's the curls, isn't it?"

"Shut up!" C. M. sneered as Sophie neared their table.

"Hey, Soph! Take a seat. How's it going?"

"Great!" said Sophie. "I can't stay. I just wanted to remind my forgetful brother to tell Mom I have play practice after school so she won't worry when I'm late coming home. We weren't supposed to have it until tomorrow, but Mr. Hunt changed it to today."

"Sure thing," said Gene. "I'll tell Mom you ran away with some stranger."

"Geeene!" Sophie moaned with a sigh. "Seriously. You heard the announcement. It won't be long."

"You're too easy to tease," Gene replied. "Sure, I'll tell Mom . . . tomorrow!"

"And, don't take too long talking to your girlfriend!" teased Sophie as she walked off.

Sophie was Gene's overachieving younger sister, who tragically (at least to Gene) was in the same grade. This meant he was unable to slack off on assignments. At least he did not have the embarrassment of her being in the same class. His friends thought she was nice-enough looking but he did not see why. To him, she was a pest, but he felt obligated to protect her, even if she resented it. Even if there was not much in their little town from which to protect her—nothing exciting ever happened.

"Hey, Gene, look out the window. That's your dad, ain't it?" asked C. M.

They all looked to where a police cruiser, lights flashing, was parked and a familiar figure was being pat down.

"No, not my dad," Gene lied.

CHAPTER 3
THE LAB

4:22 PM

Gene loved it when his father let him visit the lab. All those beakers containing who knew what chemicals, tubes circulating fluids between giant petri dishes, and lights blinking on computer panels; it all excited his imagination. He wondered what kind of experiments and discoveries he might be able to make in there. He envisioned himself in a lab coat with protective eye goggles, mixing volatile chemicals. The kind that made big explosions!

However, that afternoon he was there simply to pick up some books his father said would help him in his quest for scientific truth. His father was in a good mood, and Gene did not want to spoil it by asking why the police had pulled him over that morning. He was dying of curiosity, since as far as he knew, his father had not even received a speeding or parking ticket in years. Gene watched as his father mumbled to himself and moved paperwork to find the material he was looking for.

Gene heard a soft knock on the half-open door and watched as a young graduate student, dressed in a tan lab coat over a black T-shirt and plaid shorts, stepped timidly into the room and handed a neatly bound report to his father. With the student's one hand wrapped in clean white gauze, Gene wondered how recent his injury had been. He imagined an experiment blowing up and found himself looking for evidence of burned walls or tables. Noticing leather flip-flops, Gene smiled as he considered perhaps the guy was the typical nerd type and had tripped over his feet. He certainly looked the part with his short black hair and no facial hair, which made him look even younger than he was.

"Mr. Kysen, here's the report listing today's test results."

"Thanks, Sam. I'll look over this and get back to you about when we can start the big bang project in earnest. How's your hand?"

"It's going to leave a bit of a scar, but it doesn't hurt anymore."

"That's good . . . that it doesn't hurt. Have you met my son, Gene?"

"N-no, sir. Glad to meet you, Gene. My name is Sam . . . Sam Knisely."

He almost tripped over his flip-flops as he stepped over to shake Gene's hand.

"Sam, remember what I said about the flip-flops being taboo in the lab," said Ted Kysen.

"Sure. No problem," said Sam.

A red coloring appeared in his cheeks as he turned and left.

"What's so funny?" asked Gene when he heard his father let out a chuckle and saw him shaking his head.

"Kids these days! Doesn't anyone teach you kids to dress professionally?"

Gene knew his father preferred his assistants dress a little more professionally, as he did. He had said so many times before. Ted still wore ties, even though many of his colleagues said they were too stuffy.

"How old is he? He doesn't even look like he shaves yet," said Gene.

"He's only nineteen but already in our graduate program. He's working on his master's in physics. I asked him to assist me with testing the laser settings and strength of the experimental lab equipment. It's tricky and a little hazardous, but Sam is really good, despite the injury to his hand the other day. Sam may have a genius IQ, but he is still a kid. He reminds me of you sometimes," Ted said as he looked at Gene.

"I mean that in a good way. We've had a lot of interesting discussions from theoretical physics to religion. Sam said he used to believe in God and went to church regularly, but now he says he's outgrown that stuff. It conflicts too much with what science teaches and has proven. Do you ever feel that way, Gene?"

Gene just shrugged his shoulders. He did not want to have this discussion with his father. The truth: Gene did have lots of doubts and questions, but he just did not want to risk an argument. So he said nothing.

"That Sam used to believe and now doesn't because of his study of science greatly troubles me. I like the idea of you following in my footsteps into a career in science. I just hope it doesn't make you an atheist."

Gene shrugged his shoulders and made a face as he shook his head. Then when his father looked away, Gene rolled his eyes and let out a sigh.

"I know you complain about going to church and having family time. I guess some of that's normal. I didn't grow up in church, so I don't know. However, when I met your mother, she challenged my way of looking at life and interpreting the science I loved so much. Science brought me to God. I just don't get how it turns so many away from God."

Loud and hurried footsteps interrupted his father's musings. Damien Agnossi, lead researcher and his father's boss, came barreling into the office, slamming the door behind him. He stomped straight over to the desk.

"So, Ted, what's your excuse this time, huh? We have a deadline on this project if we want to keep the funding coming. We need some results—anything. I'm beginning to think you're purposely wasting time because you have ulterior designs for this project. You don't answer my calls; when I do get an email from you, it just says, 'Still working on it,'" he complained. "Maybe you can give this project a little priority time in your precious schedule? Some of us here actually care about our jobs and this planet we live on."

"Huh?" Ted asked as he looked up to met the angry eyes of his boss. "Can you speak a little louder? I can't hear you."

"Ted, I'm serious! What's the deal?" shouted Damien as he pointed his finger at him.

"The deal is over there in the out-basket, in that little orange envelope for the mailroom clerk to pick up. In there you'll find my report with all my time logs, what I've tried, the results, and the problem I'm trying to solve with the electromagnetic generator that keeps exhibiting very unstable characteristics every time I use it. That makes it too dangerous to adjust the laser settings. After my student helper burnt his hands working with the device, I ceased all experiments, as I detailed in my last email—yesterday, but you know that's a long time ago. I can understand if you forgot.

"As you'll recall, a portion of my job description is to ensure the safety of all personnel and university equipment. When I can ensure that, we will continue with the experiment, and not a second sooner. Also, I'm waiting for a return call from our sister lab in England. They're running some calculations for me."

Apparently, Damien did not know how to answer Gene's father. He thrust his hands into his lab coat as if to keep from pulling what was left of his hair out and stared angrily at his subordinate. Perhaps he had hoped to bully Ted into cutting some corners.

Yeah, good luck with that, thought Gene.

Damien crossed his arms and then stuck out his right hand, index finger jabbing the air.

"I hoped we'd get this experiment on track and report some results in *Science Weekly* next month. I want to be the next dean of the science department, and this experiment is my ticket to tenure. You're always so sarcastic and disrespectful. Someone needs to put you in your place, and I intend on being that someone."

Gene enjoyed watching someone else get the receiving end of his father's sarcasm. The guy never seemed to get ruffled, but he sure knew how to mess up a person's day. Gene tried not to smile as he watched Damien squirm, pinching his lips together and scrunching his nose as if he were trying to buy time to come up with the right words. Gene knew that feeling too. He always thought of great comebacks after the fact.

Damien continued his glare and snatched the envelope. He turned to leave and noticed Gene. His expression changed as he apparently had forgotten Gene was there observing everything. He left the room, slamming the door behind him. No sooner had it shut than it opened again.

Damien poked his head in and said, "Don't forget your part of the budget is due next week. I want to have a copy by Friday. I want to make sure there are no inconsistencies. This grant is too important for you to screw it up, so make sure that budget report finds its way into that yellow, er, orange envelope too!"

He left and slammed the door again. They waited and expected to hear him stomp away but noticed a small white triangle of cloth in the door. Gene smiled and cocked his head. A moment later the door opened just enough for the small sliver of cloth to disappear and closed again. When they heard his boss tread heavily into his office and slam that door, both of them let out a sigh.

Gene said, "What a jerk!"

Then he noticed a look from his father's face that made him wonder if he had forgotten he was still in the room too.

"That guy has no people skills. He makes me so angry, I can just—"

Sam re-entered the office and asked, "What was that all about?"

"The usual. He wants to hurry up the experiment and is sure we're purposely thwarting him. How can anyone like that guy?"

"Beats me, but have you seen his girlfriend? Wow—a knock-out! It gives me hope, though. If a hot girl like that can like a dweeb as childish as him, there's got to be some hottie out there for me!"

Gene smiled. He was surprised to hear another guy voice a sentiment he so often felt.

How do some of the ugliest guys at school get the hottest girls?

"Sam, there's definitely a special girl out there for you. You're a nice kid. As to how Damien ever . . . well, never mind. I've heard the rumors too. I don't know what that attractive Ph.D. candidate sees in him. It certainly can't be his personality!"

"Honestly, I hope the university finds out and boots him out of the state!"

"Now, Dad, you shouldn't judge," said Gene with mock seriousness.

Ted just glared in return. "Don't worry about him, Sam. He's just a hot-air balloon . . . that someone needs to stick with a very sharp object!"

Sam and Gene laughed.

"I see why Mom's the one in human resources and not you. Maybe you should ask her how to deal with him," Gene suggested.

"And maybe you should remember kids are to be seen but not heard!"

His father opened his eyes wide and scrunched his lips together in that way really old people do when they correct someone. Ted tried to act like he was joking, but Gene knew he was really irritated. Rifling through the papers on his desk, he looked under the orange envelope and saw the book he had been looking for.

"Here, Gene. This book will help you with that report. You can start reading while I deal with all this financial paperwork."

Gene saw a sheet of paper fall from the bottom of the envelope and drift onto the floor, unnoticed. He started to retrieve it, but his father's comment about being seen but not heard annoyed him. So he refused that little act of kindness and watched it drift silently to the floor, just under the desk.

CHAPTER 4
SECOND TICKET

6:18 PM

The ride home was uncomfortably quiet. It did not take a genius to notice Ted's foul mood.

"Can things get any worse?" he asked, holding up the ticket from the not-so-pleasant officer, who had lectured him about the dangers of speeding, especially in front of an impressionable future driver.

Gene slumped in his seat. He was not the one speeding, but for some reason he still felt guilty. He always felt guilty and wondered why: was he supersensitive, or was it because of a lifetime of hearing his father say, "Look at what you made me do"?

He knew better than to say anything, especially since that was Ted's second ticket of the day. He just hoped that day was one of the few times his mother had decided to bake. The thought of biting into a soft chocolate-chip cookie fresh from the oven helped Gene feel better.

He never told his father about his bad day, which—quite frankly—was much worse. He had gotten so wrapped up in his father's problems he almost forgot the agonizing feeling from the look on Alexis's face.

Slowly, they got out of the car and put on their game faces.

"Don't say anything to your mom about the speeding ticket. No sense messing up her day. And don't forget that book in the car. I want you to get started on that report!"

ves and went back for the book. When he walked
he overheard his parents talking in the kitchen.
of their voices, Ted was complaining about work, and
his mother, Sylvia, was doing her best to comfort him—like she always
did. As great a comforter as she was, Gene doubted even she was able
to help erase the pain of his day at school. So he decided not to tell
her either.

Gene heard Sylvia let out a sigh. He stopped and decided to eavesdrop.

"Sounds like your boss definitely has issues . . . anger issues, communication issues, and even outright jealousy."

"That's an understatement!"

"It makes me wonder if your boss isn't trying to get you off the project. Maybe he's trying to cover up something and is afraid you'll discover whatever that might be. You're very thorough, almost to the point of being obsessive."

"I'm just conscientious, but you may have a point. We disagree about almost everything. Now that you mention it, I did notice some discrepancies when I was checking over the financial report."

"Maybe you should back off a little to see if he calms down some."

"I'm not the problem. And it doesn't help dealing with this guy. I almost blew up and told him off this afternoon. He's making my life miserable! I can't wait for that other job to start."

"But that'll be sinking to his level," admonished Sylvia.

"Oh, but it'll feel so good!" muttered Ted.

"What will feel so good?" questioned Gene as he walked into the kitchen.

He dropped his backpack to the floor to use both hands to look for something good to munch on. Hunger had won out over his desire to eavesdrop any longer.

"Oh, nothing," Ted said as he turned to look at a cookie he was dunking in milk.

Gene saw his father was a little ashamed to have him overhear his vengeful thoughts. It gave him a momentary sense of pleasure.

"It'll feel good to help your mother eat that batch of chocolate-chip cookies fresh from the oven," replied Sylvia.

"Cookies? Whoa."

Gene acted more upbeat than he felt, hiding his melancholic feelings he did not want to talk about, or even acknowledge. Not yet.

"What's the special occasion? You going domestic on us, Mom? Career woman, dean of linguistics not fulfilling?"

With a smile, Sylvia replied, "It's quite fulfilling, thank you. The simple answer is I was hungry! *C'est tout!*"

"Hey, whatever. I'm not complaining. It's just what I needed," Gene said as he swiped a handful of cookies and darted for the stairs to his room.

"Oh, I forgot. Soph's got some stuff going on at school. She said she'd be a little late for dinner. Something about play rehearsals," he said and then paused a moment to look at his father with a mischievous grin. "Those red and blue lights sure are pretty and bright, aren't they, Dad?"

He ran up the stairs two at a time before his mother got in another word. He stopped momentarily and shook his head when he heard his father yell something about "that issue we still need to discuss."

He knew he should not have said anything about those lights.

Why did I do that?

More important, however, was the other "issue."

What did I do this time?

He turned to ask a question but saw the way Sylvia looked at Ted. She was obviously waiting for an explanation. Gene knew he was off the hook. So he turned, examined his cookie, and took a huge bite.

Hmm, just as good as I had imagined.

"Well," began Ted, "I kind of had a chat with a police officer about the virtues of staying within the speed limit. He wasn't impressed with my reason or my apology. I may have been a tad too open about my frustration with the city's need to fill its quotas, and, well, not only did I get a ticket, but I also got an invitation to appear in court in two weeks to tell my side of events to the presiding judge."

Sylvia just shook her head and exclaimed, "Men!"

CHAPTER 5
PRIMORDIAL MIXTURE

THURSDAY, MAY 21
10:21 PM
ASHLAND UNIVERSITY

Damien Agnossi looked up and down the hall before he quietly opened the door. He stepped inside and just as quietly closed the door, waiting a moment before he turned on the lights.

Damien had every right to be in the room, even at that time. For what he was about to do, however, it was better no one saw him. He bypassed rows of counters filled with beakers and test tubes and opened the inner door. There it was, just as he left it. That was the problem— everything was just as he left it.

He was hoping to duplicate the 1958 Stanley Miller experiment that created amino acids in the lab, thus proving Darwin's theory of evolution and establishing a divine Creator was unneeded for life to form. Since then, the experiment had been criticized for not replicating a true primordial atmosphere. No one really knew what that might have been, but scientists had since discovered it was not the mixture of methane, ammonia, and water vapors Miller had used. The hydrogen in the water vapors might have escaped into the atmosphere.

Another experiment had tried to replicate a primordial atmosphere using more carbon dioxide. It had produced organic material, but what most people did not realize was that organic material was formaldehyde or cyanide so toxic no one could breathe in the fumes without fatal consequences, it certainly couldn't spawn life!

No, what Damien hoped to do was create true amino acids: the building blocks of proteins, the building blocks of life, and the repository of information needed to continue replicating life. What he was doing in that moment was helping his experiment along.

After all, anyone with a brain knew evolution was a fact, not a theory. So eventually, someone was going to get the mix right, and that someone ought to be him—he deserved it. He had spent over twenty years teaching science and researching it. Damien had been too busy to get his work published; however, his job and whole future hinged upon it. He needed the experiment to work so he had something good . . . no, something spectacular to write about and the money that came with it.

Won't that make old Ted cringe? he thought with a laugh. *That'll make Ted shut up about there being an intelligent designer or creator—God—who decides morality and to whom mortals owe allegiance.*

No one told Damien what was right or wrong but himself. Science trumped the Bible any day. Science was the answer to everything.

But while we're evolving, we do need money. Survival of the fittest and all that!

A clap of thunder startled him.

That's right. We're supposed to have quite a storm tonight.

Damien resisted the urge to laugh out loud like a mad scientist as he poured a mixture of more favorable chemicals into his primordial atmosphere. Instead, he laughed at its irony.

CHAPTER 6
THE ASSEMBLY

FRIDAY, MAY 22
9:05 AM
LOUDONVILLE JUNIOR HIGH SCHOOL

Mr. Lyle climbed onto the platform and adjusted the microphone.

"Students! Students! Thank you for attending our little gathering here at Loudonville Junior High. Even if you weren't required to be here," he said to interject some humor, "I know you'd all be here anyways. Today we have a guest speaker, Mr. Ted Kysen, who is head physicist at Ashland University. He's here to present another great career in science, a truly remarkable field that's literally exploding with discoveries. Please welcome our guest."

Gene joined the applause with mixed emotions. He loved his father and really was impressed with how smart he was, but lately they were not as close. His mind focused more on their disagreements: his clothes, his hair cut, church, what time he had to be in. Actually, they disagreed on just about every issue, especially evolution. That year's science projects had caused Gene to have doubts about what he had been taught in church.

His father might know a lot about physical science, but biology was not his field. His science teacher majored in biology; even though his father had told him Christians should not accept evolution, Mr. Lyle made a lot of sense in class. After all, the textbook had pictures to show

33

how species evolved. Mr. Lyle said there were lots of fossils showing the in-between species. He also pointed to the numerous species of dogs that breeders created to show things changing over time.

Because of this, Gene was a little afraid his father might say something dumb about creation in front of everyone. Not because Gene did not believe in God, but like his teacher said, "Keep religion in church and science in school, and don't mix the two." His sister thought it morally wrong for their teacher to say such a thing, but she was younger and a girl.

Guys know more than girls about science. After all, aren't most scientists and science teachers guys?

Gene realized he was not paying attention when he heard everyone clapping. His father had just finished telling them what made him choose to be a scientist and what he was working on.

"Working in research doesn't pay as well as working for private industry. However, I'm fascinated by research and happy to be on the cutting edge of scientific discoveries."

So far, so good, thought Gene.

"Mr. Kysen, I understand you're currently involved with some very interesting work at the university that can advance the evolutionary model. Can you tell us a little about that work? Or is that all hush-hush?" asked Mr. Lyle.

Oh, no. Here it comes.

"Actually, some of it is quite secret. Basically, however, I'm involved with a reproduction of the Stanley Miller experiment of 1958, where Dr. Miller tried to create life in the laboratory. The biochemistry part is being conducted by my colleague, Mr. Agnossi. I'm responsible for the physics behind the generation of power for the experiment. At this point, I want to remind people that as scientists, we design experiments to test the theories others have generated.

"Many scientific findings can be interpreted to support either evolution or intelligent design or creation, depending on the scientist's philosophy. Scientists are people, just like you, who have beliefs and biases. So good science tests its theories."

"Thank you, Mr. Kysen," Mr. Lyle interrupted. "We do have a few minutes for questions. Does anyone have a question?"

"How much do you make?" asked one of the more popular kids, slouched up front.

"That's one of the secrets I told you about," answered Ted to the amusement of the audience, especially the teachers. "But it's a comfortable amount. I do have a friend who makes over $100,000 a year working for a private industry."

"Whoa!" someone voiced.

A couple students were heard saying, "Guess maybe I'll add a science class to my schedule next year . . . maybe two classes!"

"So do you work with mixing toxic chemicals?" a girl with long, silky blonde hair asked. "Do you also make sure nothing leaks into the environment to pollute it?"

"Did you ever blow anything up?" someone else shouted.

"No, never blew anything up on purpose or by accident. And, no, my colleague, Mr. Agnossi, does the biochemical experiments. I'm designing a machine to generate the precise amount of electromagnetic energy. I have also added the capacity of laser energy, using a model Dr. Ron Mallett designed for his time-travel machine, which we have discovered has applications to our experiments."

At the mention of time travel, the audience oohed and aahed, and everyone started talking. Again, Mr. Lyle took the microphone to quiet the audience.

"I think that's about all the time we have left. I see a few more hands. You there in the front row. Yes, you. Go ahead with your question."

"Mr. Kysen, we're studying evolution in science class, and I thought all scientists believed in evolution. Do you?"

"No," replied Ted before Mr. Lyle was able to take back the microphone. "I used to, but it was actually my study of science, and asking lots of questions, that made me question evolution. The facts kept pointing to a Designer, an Intelligent Designer. I believe that Intelligent Designer is the God of the Bible."

Just then a bell rang.

"Well, Mr. Kysen, I'm sorry to have to interrupt you, but that bell tells the students it's time to go. Those of you in my classes, don't forget your term papers!"

"Whew, that was close," Gene said out loud. "A minute longer and my dad woulda had an altar call!"

"What's an 'altar call?'" asked C. M. as students fled the gymnasium.

"Oh, never mind," answered Gene. He gestured wildly with his hands. Unfortunately, he hit another student with the book he held in his hand. The kid looked daggers at him. Gene started to panic as he closed his eyes and put his hands up to protect his face. This was not just any kid. It was the football captain, Ken Jarvis, who also happened to be a star wrestler in the heavyweight class. He was all too quick to prove it to anyone who provoked him.

Gene wished he did not talk so much with his hands. Surprisingly, nothing happened. When he opened one eye to see why, he noticed the gym teacher and principal standing nearby.

That was close.

Ken, rumored to have been in trouble with the cops for beating up a kid, was probably also involved in underage drinking. Gene was just thankful he had not become Ken's latest victim.

"Gee-eene, Gene," called his sister in a high, piercing voice. "Hey, Gene, Dad told me to tell you to go ahead home. He got a call from the lab . . . something about the power source acting funny. He's going to go see what's going on. They told him it was urgent."

"You going straight home or do you got play practice again?" Gene asked.

He was glad for the interruption. He did not want to continue his father's conversation about how science actually converted him to belief in God, nor was he comfortable with Ken glaring at him.

"Play practice, as usual. And Dad wanted me to make sure and tell you he wanted to see what you had on your report for Mr. Lyle's class."

Sophie waved at a friend, who emerged from the throng of students exiting the gym, and then threaded her way toward her.

Gene sighed and shook his head. His father knew about the report, which he had not started. He knew he was due to be grounded for a week. He turned toward his locker and ran into his friend, Kaleb, literally.

"Hey, man, don't you look where you're going? You coulda killed me with that hard head of yours," squawked Kaleb.

"Sorry. I was trying to knock you over—"

"*You*, knock *me* over? What are you, ninety-five pounds now?"

"No, 128 pounds . . . Gained a whole pound in just two days!"

"Your protein shakes must be working."

"You bet they are. Sorry about that."

"Hey, forget it. You going to A.'s house later?"

"No, my dad won't let me . . . said tonight's family night."

"Didn't I just hear your sister say your dad's gotta go to the lab?"

"Yeah."

"Well, tell your ma your dad canceled family night on account of having to go back to work!"

"But that'll be lying."

"Only a little . . . He's going to work, right? Said it was an emergency, which means it'll take him a long time. So he most likely will be canceling family night, even if he doesn't know it now. No sense wasting a Friday night staying at home. A.'s got the latest *Mummies III* game! Dude, we gotta go!" pleaded Kaleb.

Gene smiled as he thought about what Kaleb said.

"Your logic is irrefutable. What time are you going to pick me up?"

What his father did not know would not hurt him or, more importantly, Gene.

"Seven, and bring money for pizza and pop! Gotta have the right brain food for gaming," Kaleb said.

He turned to go, faced Gene again, and then in a strangely serious tone added, "See if you can also get C. M. to change his mind. He said something about having karate practice or a meet or whatever. I think maybe he's pushing himself too hard. You ever see some of the bruises he gets? Serious stuff, dude."

"No, but I'll give him a call if I don't see him later."

Gene headed to his locker.

All right, I finally got something to look forward to this weekend!

Unfortunately, however, no matter how well he played *Mummies III* that night, it was not going to be a good weekend. Real life was going to prove more threatening than the mummies in game land.

CHAPTER 7
SEVEN THEORIES

2:15 PM

Time to get started on that research paper, thought Gene as he headed to his last-period class. *An hour of study hall in the library should be enough to get started.*

He plopped his books next to an open computer. Gene still had not picked a topic. He liked science and was fascinated by several topics, which made it hard to stay focused on the topic at hand. He started out researching Darwin's theory of evolution, then Darwin's travels on the HMS *Beagle,* and then somehow Gene winded up thinking about time travel. He ended up sidetracked by Albert Einstein's theory of relativity—not that he completely understood it.

Einstein fascinated him, not just because of his theories. Gene wondered if he might ever end up like Einstein and come up with some really super-cool theory. Then kids would have to write reports about him. He liked learning about the man and discovering he did not always excel at everything. Gene discovered the claim that Einstein failed mathematics in school was not really true, just as President George Washington chopping down the cherry tree was not true.

Actually, Einstein got great grades, but he started out having trouble speaking. So much so that his parents took him to a doctor when he was four. He did have trouble learning foreign languages such as French.

French!

Gene remembered he had homework in that subject too. Already thirty minutes had passed and Gene had done nothing but stare at his paper and think of everything, except his topic.

I wonder if Einstein had this problem.

Okay, let's decide. Maybe I can compare creation to evolution. I'll start by reading Genesis 1 to see which area of creation I want to focus on.

Gene used to have no trouble believing there was a Creator. He had always been told God created everything. He did have a problem with the literal six-days part. That did not mesh with Earth's age. He had heard his friends at youth group talk about the Day-Age Theory or the Gap Theory to account for Earth's age.

He doubted Earth had been created in six days even if each day were a thousand years or if there were a gap between day one and day two. That still was not enough time to account for Earth's age, at least according to his textbooks, which caused him to doubt his beliefs and even his faith.

After all, if that part of the Bible isn't true, what about the rest of it?

So Gene's questions included who was right—his youth pastor or science teacher . . . his textbook or Bible? He did not want to deal with this issue, as it caused a lot of unpleasant emotions. It caused tension between him and his father, and even with some of his friends. He did not want to let go of everything he had been taught in church, but he did not want to be made fun of by his friends either.

Well, thought Gene, *I guess the only way to deal with this is to face it head on.*

He pulled a Bible out of his book bag. The only reason it was in his book bag was because he had forgotten to take it out after youth group the previous night. He made sure no one was watching, opened his Bible, and began to read chapter one of the Book of Genesis. It was all familiar to him, but for some reason the phrase about God dividing the light from the dark caught his attention.

"How can you divide light from dark?" Gene wondered aloud.

He had just read another one of Einstein's theories about light not being a wave, but little particles called photons.

How can light be divided from darkness?

Gene typed the word *light* into his search engine to get a general idea about what light really was and how it divided if there was not any sun yet. He read about the Northern Lights and thought about how cool it might be to travel to where he was able to see them. Then he read about the visible light spectrum and how it fits between ultraviolet and infrared waves on the electromagnetic spectrum.

After reading about several fascinating aspects of light, especially about how those fiber-optic lights were made, he needed a rest. So he went over to one of the more comfortable chairs and let the thoughts go around in his head. He closed his eyes and began brainstorming.

Let's see. Theory 1: God divided light and dark into night and day even though there was no sun. Maybe God is the light source, but how did He divide Himself? Try again.

Theory 2: Light bends. Maybe God bent the light so it was visible, kinda like those glow sticks.

He chuckled at the thought of God playing with glow sticks.

Theory 3: Light is visible and invisible. Maybe God divided light into frequencies shown on the chart from radio waves to visible light to gamma waves. That doesn't account for day and night.

Theory 4: Light is produced by energy or heat. Maybe that's the big bang . . . God divided atoms that produced something like an atomic explosion. After all, that's what the sun is . . . just one big nuclear explosion. But it's just one glob, not formed into a star yet, but giving off light. Hmm, possibility is there.

Theory 5: Einstein talked about antimatter—was it Einstein? Oh well, one of those scientists. Let's see antimatter and dark matter. God divided them. But then where did night and day come from? That's not it.

Theory 6: Light is associated with time. That's how we know how old a star is by how long it took its light to reach Earth. Maybe that's when God created time! Einstein talked about time travel.

Gene sat back in his chair and gazed at the overhead light.

Time travel . . . awesome! It'd be great to travel back in time! Then I can just talk directly to Darwin. I'd get an A on my report for sure.

Gene's stomach rumbled.

Or I can go with another theory. Theory 7: God had a great big knife and chopped a beam in half, putting light on one side and darkness on the other. Kinda like when I chop an apple in half. Hmm, apple . . . that sounds good. Newton liked apples. He liked to watch them fall from the trees.

Gene was about to drift off to sleep, but the thought of falling apples reminded him of falling frogs, which reminded him of Alexis. That brought back a queasy feeling in his gut. He had to find a way to talk to her and apologize. Hopefully, she was not still mad at him and would forgive him.

The bell rang.

So much for my homework! I need some downtime. Video games tonight should do the trick.

Gene crammed stuff into his backpack to not miss his ride home. Then he took out his wallet.

Yes! Just enough to cover my portion of the eats!

CHAPTER 8
GAME NIGHT

7:00 PM

Precisely at seven o'clock, an old burgundy Dodge Omni pulled up the driveway and honked. Gene was out the door before his mother changed her mind. He was thrilled; not only had she let him go with a minimal amount of pleading, but she also gave him ten dollars for pizza.

"Any problems?" asked Kaleb, who had just gotten his driving permit.

Gene was full of envy. He was younger than all his friends and had to wait another ten months to get his permit. Kaleb's older brother sat in the passenger seat with his headphones on, ignoring the two friends.

"Hey, when you're as charming as I am . . . what can I say?"

"Charming! Right!"

"Okay, convincing and studious. Mom thinks it's great we're going to work on our science reports first, saying 'I think a study group is a wonderful idea! Make sure you boys do that before you break out the games,'" said Gene, trying to mimic her voice.

"Study group? Good one," Kaleb said with a laugh.

"*Allons! Vite! Vite!*" said Gene, showing off one of the few French phrases he knew. "Before my mom changes her mind and calls me back!"

"Hey, dude, I take Spanish, so quit the French crap," Kaleb replied as he put his Omni in gear and headed to Andrew Dunbar's house. "Did you talk to C. M. about coming tonight?"

"No . . . Didn't have a chance at school."

Andrew wanted everyone to call him Ace. He was not skilled in sports, or gaming for that matter, but everyone shortened it to A. Since Andrew got good grades, A. was more fitting. It also made it more believable for his mother to think they might actually get some studying done.

Gene's parents liked this friend better than C. M., but C. M. was in several of his classes, making it easier to hang out. His mother was not too keen on him riding with new drivers, but since the house was only a few streets away, she made an exception that night.

They arrived in time to see the pizza delivery man leave. Gene's stomach growled at the sight of the pizza sign on his car. He felt starved because he had not eaten.

◊ ◊ ◊

A half-hour later, four large, empty pizza boxes littered the floor, and the trash was already full of Mountain Dew and Pepsi cans.

"How'd you get out of the house tonight?" A. asked Gene.

"I told my mom we were going to study first. Since we all have that report for Mr. Lyle coming due soon, she not only let me go, she contributed to our pizza fund," answered Gene.

"And we've been studying hard," interrupted Kaleb. "Gene, what's the minimum number of mummies that must be killed at level 3 before you get an extra life?"

"Elementary, my dear Watson. Twelve."

"Where's the secret door located in the burning house?" A. added.

"To the right of the picture of Grandpa Moses, which is the side where he holds the hay fork, for those of you who don't know your left from your right," teased Gene.

"What have you decided to do your report for science class on, Gene?" asked Kaleb.

"I'm not sure yet. How about you?"

"I'm going to write about dinosaurs and the fossil record. Your sister thinks dinosaurs and dragons are the same thing. Crazy, isn't it?"

Gene just shook his head.

"How about you, A.?"

"I started to write on the same topic as you but then decided I wanted to write about those moths, natural selection, and survival of the fittest."

"How far have you guys gotten?" asked Gene, and then mumbled a curse word because he had just been killed by Mummy Number 11. "Hey, Kaleb, you're just trying to mess with our concentration!"

"No, I'm not," Kaleb protested as he tried to keep from laughing. "I just don't want you to get in trouble with your mom for lying. You don't want that church roof to fall on your head this Sunday, do you?"

"So are you even going to write something for evolution or are you going to write about creation instead?" asked A., who occasionally went to Gene's youth group with him.

"Dunno. I haven't started yet," Gene replied. "Well, I've gotten a bunch of books from the library."

"Have you read any of them yet?" teased Kaleb.

"No, but at least I can read. Who read your books to you this time, Kaleb?" retorted Gene.

"Oh, shut up. Besides, there's plenty of stuff to cut and paste from the internet. Then you fix the font, and, ta-da, report. Report finished," Kaleb said proudly.

"You don't get good grades that way, do you, Kaleb? I think maybe I've been doing things the hard way," said A.

"Sometimes yes, sometimes no, but it gets done and in a fraction of the time you take. Gene, you never answered me—are you for evolution, or do you still believe that fairy-tale stuff from church?"

"It's not fairy-tale stuff," replied Gene defensively.

Despite his doubts, Gene hated it when Kaleb tried to make him feel stupid just for thinking there might be another valid explanation. After all, it is a major idea in science: to challenge and test theories.

"It is when the church teaches the world was made in six days and is only about six thousand years old. Carbon dating proves the earth is millions of years old! What do you say about that?" Kaleb challenged Gene.

"Well, my dad says carbon dating is flawed 'cause it measured a live fish as being ten million years old! And . . . and there's also a bunch of other facts he told me, but I forget the details. On top of that, your record for level 3 is also history by a million years. Look at my score!"

"It won't take me a million seconds to catch you." Kaleb muttered some unrepeatable words as he took the controller from Gene and began tapping buttons.

"Speaking of your dad, what do you think he had to go fix?"

"Ahh, who knows . . . Probably nothing. My dad is a perfectionist. It's just a university lab; what can happen there?"

"You never know. He can be working on top-secret stuff . . . like, like . . . lasers. Or maybe he's making a time machine!"

"Yeah, right."

"Or the lab can blow up. Lots of chemicals, right?"

"I dunno."

Gene laughed when he heard the *ka-pow* of Kaleb hitting a hidden bomb. Kaleb threw the controller at Gene and covered his face with his hands.

Gene boasted, "Ha! Game over. I win!"

CHAPTER 9
INTRUSION

SATURDAY, MAY 23
12:10 AM

Game night had been a success. Sylvia had not questioned Gene's story about study group or even noticed it was past midnight when he sneaked in the back door. She had fallen sound asleep grading papers. Ted, who was in his recliner, was also sound asleep, despite a large coffee mug on the end table next to him.

Gene prayed they would not wake up. He wanted to make it up the stairs unnoticed. He slid his shoes off. Then he tiptoed to the steps, watching to ensure his parents were asleep. Gene thought it extremely odd that his father—always a perfectionist about his appearance—had fallen asleep with his tie askew and dribble on his chin. It was also odd for his father to sleep soundly, so he had to avoid making any noise.

I wonder what went wrong at the lab. Musta been bad. Oh well, better for me.

Carefully, he placed his weight on the right part of the step to keep it from squeaking. He was unable to think of anything worse than waking his parents while he was sneaking upstairs. If he made it to bed safely, he might take Kaleb up on his offer to meet Alexis at the mall. Kaleb had assured him she was not mad at him about the frog incident. Gene wanted to apologize anyway.

Creak!

Gene froze and listened carefully. When he was sure he heard only the sounds of steady breathing, he slowly placed his foot on the next step. He put his weight on the step: no sound. Gene held his breath and repeated the process for each step. It was agonizing to go so slowly, but Gene did not relish the idea of ruining the night, caught when he was so close to his room—grounded forever if they woke up.

When he finally made it to his room, he felt so wiped out he only managed to remove his socks before he fell onto the bed—still fully dressed—and fell asleep. However, it was a restless sleep.

His dreams featured visions of lightsabers, and exploding stars and loud bangs to go with them. In his dream, he saw his father's lab explode: fire was everywhere. He looked for his father but was unable to see anything in the dark, thick smoke. He tried to call for his father but was unable to speak. He tried harder and woke up.

He felt a sudden pang of fear as he wondered if something did happen to his father. No, he had been in the recliner when Gene came home. He fell back into another dream: more noises, yelling. A sharp *crack* brought him to full consciousness—at least he thought he was fully awake.

As he scanned his room, the dresser started to move, and a black shadow approached him. He felt utter panic creep into every part of his being. Then the shadow morphed into a neon-green frog with its guts missing—like the one his class had tossed around the science classroom, only freaky looking.

It was saying something to him. He listened harder as it asked, "Where's my missing link?"

Gene should have known he was dreaming at that point, but he simply answered the frog. "I didn't take it."

The frog morphed back into a sinister shadow; it stomped and thumped on the walls. Red lasers and lightning flashed. He knew he was dreaming but was unable to wake up.

Thump . . . thump . . . crash!

Gene was unable to move or speak. He heard noises again: thuds, bumps, yelling.

How many times am I going to have this dream before I finally wake up?

He felt paralyzed and helpless. His eyes popped open. Every nerve in his body was on full alert.

Am I awake or still dreaming?

He listened and heard the noise again: a loud thud, yelling. Adrenaline zipped through his body like electricity when he realized he was not dreaming anymore. The noise was real. Someone *had* been banging on the door. Panic filled his heart again. He had to force himself to breathe slowly.

Someone, actually several someones, were in his house.

Which door had they come in? Where are they? Are they near my room?

Gene wanted to cry out for his parents.

There was another thud at the back door to his house!

Who in the world is at that door in the middle of the night and making such a racket?

His parents were downstairs.

Are they okay?

Suddenly, there were bright lights shining in the house. Then people were yelling.

Dad? Mom?

They were yelling, but so were a bunch of voices he did not recognize. For a moment he did not know whether to pull the blankets over his head, hide under the bed, or go help—at least see what was going on.

His heart raced. His breathing was rapid. His mouth was dry.

I can't stay here, he thought as he mustered up courage from deep inside. *I gotta find out what's going on. No way am I going to let some intruder attack Mom and Dad!*

As his heart still raced, he jumped up to look for a weapon. He spied his favorite heavy-hitter bat, grabbed it, and ran to the stairs. The weight of the bat gave him courage.

Gene descended the first flight of stairs as quickly and quietly as possible. As he turned the corner to descend the rest of the stairs, he froze mid-step.

A gun pointed at him!

CHAPTER 10
HIDING PLACE

SATURDAY, MAY 23
3:23 AM

The bright red and blue lights had finally stopped flashing. Charles Darwin peeked out of the closet he had hidden inside. Everything was so strange, even eerie, in the darkness. He felt queasy and jittery, as if he had been hit by lightning, although he was not quite sure how that felt. One minute he had been looking for his coat.

Now I'm . . . here . . . wherever here is.

Slowly, his memory returned, but the sights he remembered did not make sense.

Maybe I'm just dreaming?

Darwin rubbed his face with both hands but discovered it was painful. He felt a wet spot that was not perspiration. He tried to find some light to examine his head.

His eyes still tried to readjust, as he had been exposed to a brilliant light surrounding him. Yet there were only smaller lights of unusual colors that currently surrounded Darwin. As his surroundings came into focus, he saw the form of another person. At first, he assumed it was his friend. When he did not recognize the man, he assumed him to be another scientist he had not met that night.

"Excuse me, my good man, but can you—"

Before Darwin finished his question, the other man started to scream wildly. The events that followed were a blur; everything happened so fast. Darwin had no time to absorb it all; he just retreated back into the closet and kept trying to understand what had just taken place.

Who was that man? What had caused him to scream so hysterically, as if he'd seen some ghostly phenomenon?

Darwin wondered if perhaps it was blood all over his head.

What's that contraption with all the strange, blinking lights?

It had to have been at least seven feet high. It had tubes and beakers with a reddish-brown fluid circulating throughout. Thinking of the strange machine, he wondered if maybe it was all a dream. Yet his senses told him it was real.

But where am I?

Until he was able to figure out where he was, perhaps it was prudent to stay hidden. Then again, that man may need assistance.

I should go help.

Darwin's head pounded and his stomach hurt again. He was not sure he was able to move.

This night is going to send me back for another six months of treatment, for sure!

CHAPTER 11
OVERKILL

3:28 AM

Gene stared in stunned disbelief.

Am I still dreaming?

It was not just one gun or one person, but a lot of them armed with automatic rifles and all dressed in black. Even their faces were covered. They were shouting something, but he couldn't understand them.

So many thoughts and emotions raced through his head in that moment. First, confusion, then fear, even humor—he thought he had to be dreaming—and then back to fear. He did not know how it was possible to feel the need to fight and flee simultaneously. It was as if the synapses in his brain raced around in every direction so no signals went to his arms or legs. He was incapable of any movement, afraid to even take another breath of air.

He saw his mother, noticed the fear in her facial expression, watched her mouth move, but was unable to understand her words. Everyone seemed to move in slow motion. His gaze settled on his father, who lay prone on the floor as two men restrained him while another pinned handcuffs on him.

Handcuffs?

Gene was really confused by then.

Why is the army here? Why are they handcuffing Dad?

Then he heard someone yell, "Police!"

53

Why are they here?

At that moment, Gene realized they were yelling at him!

He heard himself blurt out, "Isn't this kinda . . . like . . . overkill?"

He heard several commands issued to him, but he did not know whose to listen to.

"Just drop it, Gene!" his mother yelled, bringing him out of the trance.

He realized he was still holding his baseball bat and the officers were yelling at him.

"Drop the bat and put your hands up!"

So he did. He dropped the bat, which seemed to have a mind of its own as it rolled down the stairs in slow motion into the officers. He wanted to yell "No!" but nothing came out.

The next thing he knew, he was on the floor with not one but three officers on top of him! He did not even remember coming down the stairs. He felt a handcuff go on one wrist.

Why? What?

Then an officer pulled on his other arm, but it was stuck under his body. With two officers on top of him, it was not budging!

"I can't move it!" Gene yelled.

"Don't resist arrest! Give me your hand."

"I can't move it!" Gene yelled again. "Get off of me . . . You're hurting me!"

Finally, the officers got off of him. His hand easily came out from under him and it was promptly cuffed. Gene was confused.

Did the officer just say I was under arrest?

CHAPTER 12
IN CUSTODY

4:30 AM

The bright lights contrasted so much with the dark night, Gene's eyes hurt. The handcuffs were so tight, Gene was sure he might never be able to use his hands again. At least he had an excuse to not write his report. That was the least of his worries at the moment. In the back of a police car, unsure about where he was going, or even why, he desperately tried to make sense of what had just occurred.

Why are they arresting Dad? Did they arrest Mom too? What about Sophie?

His anxiety increased as the police car pulled into a brightly lit garage. When the squad car stopped, one of the two officers in the front seat opened his door and reached over to undo his seatbelt. Finding it already undone, the officer held up the loose end.

"Trying to escape already?"

"No, sir. It was jabbing me in the side, and I wanted to lie down. So I undid it."

"Uh-huh. Well, from this point on you better not burp unless we say so. Got it?"

Gene was so intimidated by the officer, he was barely able to squeak out, "Y-yes, sir."

The officer undid the handcuffs and made Gene stand up against the squad car with his hands and legs spread out. Then he began to pat Gene down.

◊ ◊ ◊

It was large inside. Several more police officers stood inside, glaring at him.

"Got anything in your pockets?"

"Uh, I don't think so."

"Turn your pockets inside-out."

Gene obeyed. He had $1.23, a pencil stub, and a folded piece of paper. At first, he was unsure what was on the paper. Kaleb had given it to him. Another officer took the paper and unfolded it.

"'The mall food court, 11:00 A.M. Be there.' Well, I doubt you'll make that appointment. Hope it's not a hot date."

Gene just stood still, but inside his stomach the butterflies were growing by the second, his knees were shaking, and his hands were sweaty.

How long will I be here? And, yes, it is a hot date.

Kaleb had called one of Alexis's friends last night, who told him they were going to be at the mall the next morning. Gene had been so excited. Once again, his plan to meet Alexis was not going to work out.

Is there some kind of cosmic force against us ever getting together?

"This way."

An officer held open a door and Gene went inside where it was cold. He did not have a chance to see much else, as someone opened another door and urged him forward.

It was a dingy, yellow, cement-brick room with one long cement bench. The room was about the size of his bedroom minus all his stuff. There was a cement wall about three feet high with a toilet behind it. There was a big window in place of the wall on one side, so he was able to see the officers at their desks.

Well, it's probably so they can see me.

His anxiety level was still high.

Why did this have to happen tonight?

He did not feel like sitting down. He wanted to do something, had to do something. After pacing for what seemed like hours but had probably only been a few minutes, Gene sat down. He was cold; even his feet were cold. For the first time, he noticed he had no shoes or socks on.

"Sheesh," he muttered. "No shoes. No watch. Nothing to do; I'm going to go crazy, bonkers, to the mental ward!"

He wanted to shout for someone to let him out before he did lose it completely but decided against it. Even schoolwork sounded interesting compared to his predicament.

Gene looked to see what was going on outside his little cell. They were bringing in someone else. As they turned the kid around to take off his handcuffs, Gene recognized him.

Oh great! I hope they don't put him in here with me!

CHAPTER 13
THE CRIMINAL

Six hours later, Gene was in the back of the family car, and his mother was still crying.

Sophie kept repeating, "I can't believe it. I can't believe it . . . Dad wouldn't . . . he couldn't . . . No way . . . No way!"

Gene spent five and a half hours at the youth detention facility before he was released. He finally found out why the SWAT team was at his house. He wished he had been a coward and hid under his bed.

Maybe this was one of those long dreams you keep thinking you'll wake up from, but don't.

The aches in his back, arms, and head told him it was not true. The bench in his cell was hard concrete. Not only was sleep impossible, but his back was also in knots. He had a nice bruise on his left forearm and another on the left side of his head after being slammed to the floor. He was still unsure how he got from the steps to the floor; he was even unsure what he had done wrong.

As he reflected on the events of the night and being booked, he did not know whether to laugh or cry. It was all so extreme, so bizarre . . . He had a criminal record! Him, the kid always teased because he was never able to go out with the gang. The one who felt guilty for telling his mother a half-truth and sneaking in only a half-hour after curfew!

When the police finally released him to his mother, he was so tired of doing nothing even homework sounded exciting. When he was being released, he saw the kid from school again. He was mouthing something to Gene, but Gene was not able to understand what he was saying. He was unsure he wanted to know.

What nice thing could Ken Jarvis have to say to me?

Unfortunately, Ken saw him. Even worse, he recognized him and smiled—a sneer really. Gene was unsure if that was good or bad. At first, he had been horrified, but then he wondered if it might be good. Ken actually seemed impressed and had given Gene thumbs up and smiled again.

"Hey, DNA!"

DNA? Why'd he call me that? Maybe because my name is Gene?

Then he remembered some kids started calling him that during the biology unit when he correctly answered a question about genetics no one else knew. He was surprised he had gotten it right because he had been daydreaming. The teacher had called his name three times before he answered.

It was probably Kaleb who started that. Kaleb was always ribbing him about something. He said DNA also stood for *Does Not Answer*.

What nickname will Kaleb give me after this?

Then he remembered they were supposed to meet at the mall.

What will Kaleb and Alexis think when I don't show?

He was unable to even get to a telephone to let them know what was going on. He started shaking his foot and tapping his fingers. There had to be a way to get to the mall. He knew it was useless to ask his mother; she looked so tired.

His intense anxiety started to wear off and resignation replaced it. The meeting was not going to happen.

Not today, probably not ever. This whole thing is so unfair!

Gene had been so lost in his thoughts that when the car stopped, he assumed they were home. He was surprised to see they were at the local emergency center.

"Why are we here?" he asked as a sudden sense of panic rose inside. "Is Dad here?"

"No," his mother said, but then after a moment, with a determined look, she added, "I don't know much about the law, but I know you got a nasty bruise on your head, and I want two things. First, to make sure you're okay and second, to get evidence of how roughly you were handled."

"But I need to get to a phone first," Gene protested.

"Absolutely not. We need to get you checked out right now!"

Sophie added, "I can't believe they did this. This is America. We're innocent until proven guilty, right? How can they just arrest Dad and Gene like this?"

"Apparently not," Sylvia answered. "They said they had a warrant. Apparently, that lets them do whatever they want. They won't even tell me why they arrested your father. They just told me it was deadly serious and I needed a lawyer as soon as possible. It wasn't until I was getting you out when I overheard two officers mention 'the kid whose dad was arrested for murder.' I'm not even sure they were talking about you."

"So you still don't even know what Dad was arrested for?" Gene asked.

His mother just shook her head and wiped a tear off her cheek.

"So what was I charged with? I wasn't paying attention when they told me. I just wanted to get out of there."

"Let's see: obstructing official business, resisting arrest, and assault of a police officer."

"My brother, the criminal," Sophie stated, shaking her head.

"Well, I got something to talk about at school on Monday," quipped Gene.

He tried to lighten the mood with his comment. He saw how upset his mother was. Even though he agreed with his sister's outrage, he wished she would just be quiet.

"Gene, I have to caution you it may be better that you don't say anything. I haven't talked to a lawyer yet, but you're still facing charges that are pretty serious. And I know when the police say, 'Anything you say can and will be used against you in a court of law,' they mean it. You remember my friend, Jill, at the school, don't you? Her son had a horrendous time getting his charges dropped because someone in his class told the prosecutor what he said while he was bragging and joking with his friends. I don't remember what the charge was, but Jill was a wreck for quite some time."

⌂ ⌂ ⌂

Sylvia finally had time to take stock of her situation.

What a night!

She allowed herself to go over the night's events again. One minute she had been sleeping cozily on her sofa, and the next her husband was lying on the floor with his hands cuffed, two officers pinning him to the floor. Before that registered in her sleep-deprived state, Gene had come down the stairs with a bat, ready for battle. He was obviously thinking a burglar or worse was in the house.

Poor kid, he was just trying to defend his family!

Unfortunately, the police did not see it the same way. Before she could even scream, "Don't!" they had him in cuffs too! Then to make matters worse, it was Friday night and she had just discovered her checking account was empty. Even a second try yielded the message: Denied, Insufficient Funds.

What was I to do?

Her husband and son were in jail, and she still was not even sure why. She had no money to bail them out, and the jail only took cash. It was too late to contact a lawyer.

What lawyer should I contact? It's not as if I ever had a need for a lawyer, let alone a criminal lawyer!

Overwhelmed at the thought of finding a lawyer, she felt herself shutting down.

A double latte from Starbucks would be nice, but I don't even have money for that.

So there was only one thing to do. Stop by the store and get a half-gallon of chocolate-chip, cookie-dough ice cream with the five dollars she had and then go home and eat the whole container.

She wanted to throw a fit—a royal temper tantrum, but she had her daughter with her. So she had to be the adult.

Do kids ever appreciate how hard it is to be an adult? Kids can throw a fit. Actually, it's expected of them . . . But adults? No, we have to act responsibly.

"Hey, Mom," Sophie interrupted. "Are we going to be on the news?"

Sylvia's eyes widened. She had not considered it. She did not even want to think about it. She wanted to scream, but she calmed herself.

She replied, "There's no way to tell. I sure hope not, but I won't make you go to school on Monday, if you don't want to."

"Are you kidding . . . I want to go!" said Sophie. "Nothing exciting ever happens to us. I want to tell my friends what happened."

Sylvia looked at her daughter, started to say something, and thought better of it.

"Let's just get some ice cream and chocolate syrup . . . lots of it."

"Yeah," Sylvia added and then in a small, serious voice said, "Mom, I saw your ATM balance. I've got money in my account you can have."

CHAPTER 14
EMOTIONAL ROLLER COASTER

Three hours later, Gene was slumped in the backseat of Sylvia's car again, headed home with some prescription painkillers. The doctor said he may have a bad headache but was otherwise okay according to the x-rays . . . physically, at least. The doctor warned him he might have "psychological ramifications." In other words, his emotions might take him on a roller-coaster ride. It was a good thing he liked roller coasters.

He thought he was doing okay dealing with the emotional trauma of the night. That is, until he saw his house. The adrenaline buzz of the night had disappeared. All the bravado he had tried to show to others was gone. All that remained was a feeling of loss and knowing something had changed forever.

It seemed so normal and yet different at the same time. Yesterday he had taken for granted that he was safe in his house and his father was going to always be there. Yet he found it hard to breathe and felt a nervous twitch in his foot at the thought of going back into his house. He felt violated.

It did not matter that it was the police and not a bunch of thieves who broke into his house. That actually made it seem worse. He had an idea police were supposed to behave a certain way.

They're not supposed to burst into your house and accuse you of something you didn't do.

The house looked the same on the inside—almost the same. A lamp was knocked over. Gene shuddered. He did not want to be in his house. He was embarrassed his teachers might soon know he had been arrested, but he was dying to tell his friends about everything that had happened.

"Mom, is it okay if I just sleep downstairs? I really don't feel like going up those stairs again," said Gene meekly as he tried to hide he was really afraid.

"Sure. I doubt I'll sleep much, despite being up all night. My body is worn out, yet my mind is racing like a runaway locomotive. It was quite the ordeal getting you out of that place, and they won't even let me talk to your dad.

"Everything is still kinda fuzzy. Nothing's making sense. One minute I was sleeping on the couch, the next I was rudely awaken by knocks at the door and shouts—I was so disoriented. Then I had to stand by, in utter confusion and astonishment, and watch the most precious men in my life arrested! I had no idea why . . . I still don't understand it."

"I thought I heard the phone ring too," said Sophie.

"Yeah, it did. That was strange. Someone asked if Theodore Kysen was at home. As soon as I said yes, he hung up," replied Sylvia.

She put her purse and keys on the kitchen counter and then went into the living room and plopped on the couch. Sophie sat down next to her mother and put her arms around her. Each had tears trickling down her cheeks. Finally, Sophie was quiet. Gene felt almost guilty for being annoyed at her when he saw the tears and sadness in Sophie's face.

His problem was tiny compared to the problem his father was facing. The police had charged him with murder! That was not for certain, according to his mother.

Do they send in a SWAT team for anything less?

Gene did not need to hear more to know it was not true.

It can't be true. No way did Dad murder anyone.

Gene felt the muscles in his jaw tighten as anger rose inside him. Not just anger, but outrage. His stomach muscles were so tight he felt he might puke. His whole body began to tremble, and his fingers moved as if they had a mind of their own. He wanted to release his pent-up anger . . . to smash something.

Instead, he took a deep breath and let it out slowly. He needed to calm down, but his mouth was still clenched shut. He wanted justice, real justice, and he fumed at who he deemed *the jerks* who had falsely accused his father.

Gene decided to do whatever was possible to discover what had really happened. There had to be something he was able to do. Maybe kids only came up with the answer in the movies, but he was going to try something . . . anything!

There has to be a way! Maybe something happened at the lab.

His father kept getting calls about problems.

What if something, or someone, blew it up?

If he was not a kid and had a license to drive, he could go check out the lab. He sighed and was about to give up hope that there was anything he possibly was able to do when an idea began to form in his mind.

It just might work if I have the courage to do it.

CHAPTER 15

ARTISTIC INTERPRETATION

Gene had no idea how long he sat in the recliner fuming. As he thought about his idea, he found a calm-feeling surface.

The house was quiet. Sylvia and Sophie had fallen asleep huddled together on the sofa. He was glad someone was able to sleep, but he was still too wound up. He tried to sort out the events of the night. He knew he had quite a story to tell his friends.

He looked at the clock and thought about calling C. M. or Kaleb. He reached for the telephone on the end table, but remembering his mother's warning about not talking to his friends until he talked to a lawyer, he let his hand drop.

Gene felt his stomach rumbling. He reasoned the medicine must be calming him enough to feel his hunger. So he made some hot chocolate and helped himself to a couple of giant oatmeal-cream cookies.

He saw the pile of stuff he had brought back from the hospital. On top was a book he had discovered and taken from the waiting room. It was an interesting-looking book on evolution. With nothing else to do, he picked it up and started leafing through the book's pages. It looked interesting and was exactly what he needed for his science report. An aide had told him someone left the book and he was free to take it if he wanted it. So he did.

He thought he might be able to focus enough on the new book to take his mind off of the previous night. It was entitled *Fact or Fiction? A Case for the Facts of Creation (and the Fiction of Evolution)*. It seemed like it might help him with the doubts he was having about creation. Yet what had really caught his attention were the pictures in the chapter called "Famous Icons." He recognized them from his science textbook.

In the comfort of his house and too wired to sleep, he started to read the chapter with the pictures that had caught his attention. It was not just the pictures that captured his imagination but also the caption "Famous Icon—Lie or Misrepresentation of the Truth?" that caught his attention.

This looks like good information for my report!

It was weird how the excitement and commotion of their arrests had taken minutes yet had been followed by endless hours of monotonous waiting. Since he had nothing else to do but think while in the juvenile jail, Gene had thought about his report. Not just because it was due soon but also because he had struggled with the arguments against evolution he had been taught in church and by his parents. He needed to figure out what he believed.

He wanted to believe in God, but he felt if evolution was really true, it meant trouble for God.

How can I trust the Bible?

His teacher had said it was full of lies and myths and had a lot of historical errors. He and his father had a lot of discussions, even arguments, about evolution. With the possibility of never seeing his father again, he had to face this crossroads on his own. Gene was so confused he did not know what he believed.

All he knew was if there was a God, he wanted His help. He still believed in God. He had plenty of time to think as he sat on that cold, cement bench in the ten-by-ten-feet room. He knew the room's size because he had paced it several times. He had prayed for a lot of things: protection, a warm blanket, and for God to get him and his father out.

He had gotten out, but Ted had not. Despite the tension between him and his father, Gene missed him already. He needed him out of jail. He needed his father.

He shuddered, stood up, and shook himself as if shaking that memory out of his mind. He noticed his hot chocolate was already gone, so he made some more. That, of course, meant getting more oatmeal cookies. He took the last one and headed back to the recliner and opened his book.

Gene had learned he sometimes tricked himself into studying. First, he opened his textbook and simply read chapter titles and subtitles. Then he looked at the pictures, which prompted him to read about them. Next, he actually began to read the text.

The first picture that caught his attention as he flipped through the pages was captioned "The March of the Ape Men: From the Java Man to the Nebraska Man." It was a drawing that showed the gradual changes from ape to man. It really made a convincing argument for evolution. After all, he saw the changes from an ape to a man, and scientists had found bones in different layers, dating them with scientific radiometric dates. However, the author said the only bone fragment of Nebraska man was a tooth later discovered to be a pig's tooth!

The author also showed pictures other artists had made from the same bones. Some looked more apelike, but they were all the same bones. Gene had often wondered how scientists were able to discover what a creature looked like from a few bones. He thought they took special measurements, but he wondered how much came from the imagination of the artist. If Nebraska man's tooth was really a pig's tooth, Gene wondered how many other bones were not really what scientists claimed them to be. Maybe the scientists were not as smart as he thought, or as smart as they thought.

He picked up a pen and looked for some paper. He saw a discarded envelope lying on the end table. He made sure it was empty and began writing notes.

Scientists aren't always right. Drawings are up to the artist's imagination and so may not be accurate.

Then he wrote the page number and continued reading. Next, he turned to the picture of the archaeopteryx, the classic evolutionary proof of the in-between stage of reptiles and birds. It was what he thought to be a really cool-looking bird. However, that icon also had problems. The bird later became an extinct species. Gene wondered why that fact was not in textbooks. He made a note of this too.

Gene had become really curious and was a little ticked off that his textbooks were biased. However, that was only two examples, so he turned to the chapter on Haeckel's embryos. The picture showed the similarities in early embryos as they develop. There was a fish, salamander, tortoise, chick, hog, calf, rabbit, and human . . . and they all looked similar.

Pretty convincing proof, thought Gene.

Then his jaw dropped in surprise and he shouted, "No way!"

CHAPTER 16
GILLS AND WOODCUTS

"Incredible!" said Gene at the shocking news. "Of all the double-crossing hoaxes . . ."

He was having trouble believing the author's claim. Even worse, textbook publishers knew about it for almost one hundred years.

Is this the reason evolution sounds so good in school?

Textbook authors deliberately made sure the evolutionary theory did not fail.

Even if it means doing this? I gotta check this out.

He stood and searched the usual spots where he often left his backpack. He found it by the door, unzipped the main compartment, and took out his science textbook. Its binding was weak from all the homework papers stuffed inside. Gene returned to the recliner, got comfortable, and flipped through the pages.

Yep. There they are—Haeckel's embryos.

Gene quickly glanced at the subtext under the pictures. There was no indication there had been anything new discovered to refute these findings. He took a deep breath and let it out slowly and deliberately. This discovery angered him.

How can textbooks deliberately deceive us like this!

He looked back at the new book and at the photographs taken with newer ultrasound technology, which showed distinct differences.

No way they're similar!

Gene started pacing. He wanted to go tell his mother about this horrible deception, but he knew she was already distraught from the occurrences of the previous night. He decided to wait, but he was definitely going to talk to his science teacher to complain.

Heck, I'll tell the principal and write the school board! This is outrageous—if we can't trust our textbooks, who can we trust? Why do I have to memorize this stuff if it isn't even true?

The more Gene read, the more he paced. The more he paced, the angrier he became.

The book had a picture of a human embryo with an arrow pointing at the neck area. It had a caption that read, "What about those gills?"

Yeah, what about those gills?

He was suspicious of all the proof he had gathered in his science notebook. The author suggested the reader bend his head with his chin on his chest and then feel his neck. It read, "Feel those folds?" That was what the ultrasound showed—folds from the bent head.

They definitely aren't gills!

"They're just a bunch of liars!" Gene said.

He plopped down in his recliner and threw his hands in the air in disgust. However, the book was in his hand and went sailing across the room. Gene watched the book as it seemed to soar in slow motion. He cringed and looked away, fearing it might hit his sleeping mother.

"Ouch!" yelled a sleepy Sophie. "Why'd you do that? Who're the liars? I didn't say anything!"

"Sorry," said Gene as he retrieved his book.

Actually, he was relieved it only hit his sister. Still, he was surprised the book sailed like that. Good thing he had not actually thrown his bat.

"Gotta quit talking with my hands. Hey, while you're up, bend your head forward."

"What? Why?"

"Just do it. I want to show you something."

"First you throw a book at me, and then you want me to bend my head forward. Have you gone crazy?" Sophie shook her head in pity.

"Come on; bend your head forward like this."

Gene bent his head. Sophie let out a sigh of disgust, but she bent her head forward as requested.

"Okay, now what?"

Gene touched the folds in her neck and said, "Feel that? It's certainly not gills."

"I never said they were gills," Sophie said slowly as if to someone mentally challenged.

"I know you didn't, but look here. See that picture?"

"Yeah. So what?"

"This is the book I picked up at the hospital to help me with my report. It's got all kinds of stuff in it about how our textbooks are lying to us. That picture there is pointing to what some evolutionists call gill slits in human embryos, but it's nothing of the sort."

Sophie read the picture description and said, "Doesn't surprise me."

"Well, look at these pictures of Haeckel's embryos. They're in our textbook . . . I checked. This book says they're nothing but fakes and our textbook publishers know it!"

"That's fraud. We should tell someone," said Sophie who was also getting upset. "What else does it say? This is really getting interesting."

"They say Haeckel actually used the same woodcut for each embryo, but those photos from actual ultrasounds of each animal embryo show they're nothing like the pictures in our books . . . and look at this."

Gene turned to the next picture. It displayed four mammals' appendages: a human arm, bat wing, dolphin fin, and horse leg.

"It says the similarity between human bone structure and other animals—called morphology—is often used to prove evolutionary descent. In reality, all it means is they're alike. It can mean a common designer."

Gene looked at his sister. "I never thought of it like that, but it makes sense."

"Makes plenty of sense to me," said Sophie. "Hey, look at this picture."

Sophie pointed to a picture of Darwin's tree of life showing how animals branched off from each other. She read the dark print under it.

"'Many modern scientists now think of the descent as blades of grass, not a tree. The fossil record does not show gradual changes that branch out like a tree. It shows sudden, drastic changes, with all the animal types appearing at once, fully formed.' That's just what our pastor says."

"Yeah, he does. Wow!" said Gene.

He was angry at being lied to, but fascinated there actually was support for creation. He kept reading the text, not just the picture labels. Sophie read over his shoulder.

He had read about the Cambrian explosion but did not realize it might actually be more beneficial to a creation model than evolution. The Genesis flood, being catastrophic and worldwide, might have caused many of the fossil deposits, especially the one in Utah where he had once gone on a Boy Scout trip. There they had unearthed dozens of jumbled dinosaur fossils seemingly pieced together. Exactly what a person expected from a cataclysmic, worldwide flood.

Sophie said, "Looks like proof for creation or at least good evidence."

"Yeah. When I hear evolution taught in school, it always sounds like there's no support for creation. Like you have to be stupid to believe there's a God who created the world."

"Hey, look at this picture. Looks like the experiment Dad is working on!"

Sophie tried to take the book from her brother, but he wrestled it back. He read the information under the picture of the cool-looking lab—the kind Dr. Frankenstein might have used. It was the Stanley-Miller experiment where they claimed to have made life in the lab.

Actually, what they made was . . .

"Cyanide," Gene and Sophie exclaimed in unison.

"That's certainly not very helpful for starting life," said Sophie.

They jumped when they heard their mother say, "Huh? Sayonara to you too."

Sophie and Gene looked at each other, and then at their mother. They had forgotten she was sleeping on the sofa. When they were sure they had not awakened her, they let out a sigh of relief. Neither of them wanted to be responsible for waking their mother out of such a calm, peaceful sleep.

"Sayonara?" whispered Gene.

He started to laugh. Sophie covered her mouth as if that might contain her laughter.

"Uh-hum, back to the book," she said in mock seriousness.

Gene opened the book to the picture of the lab experiment and laughed again. The picture was especially interesting because his father was involved with an experiment like this one at the college. He needed to talk to his father about it when he got out of jail.

If he gets out.

The thought instantly sobered him.

"Was that what happened at the lab? They made cyanide and someone got killed?" Gene wondered out loud.

He felt his mood darken again. If that was, in fact, what had happened, he knew it had to be an accident. His father might be a mean disciplinarian and a perfectionist, but he was not a killer. Gene wanted to do something so badly. He stood up and started to pace again.

Sophie said, "I'm sure that's not it, but it sure will be nice to know. Wasn't this the experiment Dad and his boss were copying, or trying to copy?"

"Yeah, I sure wish I could do something to help Dad out," said Gene.

He tried in vain to think of something to do. He remembered his idea, but he had to wait before he acted on it. There was nothing he could think of to help his father at the moment. Out of frustration, he kicked a pillow that had fallen off the sofa.

Thinking about his father reminded Gene about how he had actually been glad Ted had a rough night so he could sneak in without getting into trouble. He felt guilty about it. He sat down and thrust his hands behind his head.

"Sheesh," he thought out loud. "After these strange events, I think a chewing out is so much better!"

He found himself staring off into space. He wanted to put all the mess out of his mind.

"I know how you feel. I so badly want to help, but everyone just keeps ignoring me."

"Better to be ignored than arrested."

"I guess you're right about that."

Gene watched Sophie's expression sadden. He knew his despair was affecting her. It seemed to make her angry and sad at the same time. She sat in the desk chair and slumped over as she released a sigh. They were both quietly lost in their own thoughts.

"Well, I finally feel tired enough to sleep," said Gene.

"Then I'll go to my room to sleep. It's safer there. I only got up to go to the bathroom anyways. Next time I'll know to watch for flying books. Try to get some sleep."

Sophie half-smiled at her brother and left the room. Then Gene heard her come back. He looked up to see what she wanted. He saw her smile and quietly place the envelope with Gene's notes back on the end table.

"Sayonara," she whispered.

He smiled and shook his head.

He looked at the book he had been reading. Then he glanced at the clock. He had a lot of thinking to do. That book had challenged everything he had been taught about evolution. The SWAT invasion challenged his belief in a just legal system.

So what's true anyway?

It seemed like everything in his life was in an uproar, and he was not even allowed to talk to his friends about any of it. There was something he had to talk to Kaleb about, but he could not recall what it was about. He was getting so tired his thoughts were jumbled.

Then Haeckel's embryos and the Stanley-Miller experiment pictures came back into his mind. He wanted to learn more about them. Yet as interesting as the book was, he was not going to get any more reading done. Gene's thoughts drifted back to his father. All he thought about was him still in jail.

How's he doing? Why did this have to happen?

The pain medicine made him very drowsy. He yawned and stretched and then pushed the recliner to its full recline position. He tried to read some more, but he fell asleep with the book open and the light on.

CHAPTER 17
PROSECUTOR'S OFFICE

SATURDAY, MAY 23
4:05 PM

"You had better hope he dies!" yelled Paul Mangil, the city prosecutor.

He had an angry scowl on his face as he ordered the detective into his conservatively decorated office. He shut the door to drown out office noise.

"Because if he doesn't, we may have a huge lawsuit on our hands! As I go over this report again, I'm not sure it was wise to go after the professor like that, Sal. I thought you said the Agnossi guy was dead!"

"I was at the hospital when I called you, and you were okay with everything then," replied Sal. "I told you, all I saw for sure was the doctor shake his head like his patient had just passed. So don't accuse me of any wrongdoing. I'm sure it was the right thing to do. We found some pretty convincing evidence at the scene. The professor's name was written on the floor in blood!

"I mean, the other professor may not be dead yet, but I'll bet he'll be before this day is over. I heard the doc say he'd flatlined once, and he's in a coma; the docs aren't convinced he'll come out of it. Matter of fact, I heard them ask for his next of kin."

"Almost dead isn't the same as dead."

"Anyway, I figured I was not gonna let this perp get away. Not this time . . . No one is gonna flee the country on me again," Sal continued.

"Besides, my gut says that killing was the professor's ultimate goal—trust me, I know. I been in this business long enough to know. I've seen lots of perps who had everyone else fooled with their pretenses of being the outstanding citizen."

Paul shouted, "But he's a deacon in his church!"

"Don't matter. They can kill as easy as anyone else. It's all a front."

"And you're sure *Ted* is what was written in blood? Have you got blood samples?"

"Come on, Paul. You know me. I know my job."

"Well, as the city prosecutor, I've got to make sure you follow the book so we don't get sued!" Paul replied. "At least we have to prove we acted within standard procedures."

Paul had only been the city's prosecutor for a year, but he did aspire to higher office in bigger cities. Although Sal Cozens was usually on target with his hunches, he had become a little sloppy with his reports. Paul was not too worried if his detectives and police slightly stepped over the line to get a bad guy, but he did not want it so obvious that he might lose the case. Nor did he want any bad attention from the public media.

"Don't worry, kid. You're the best," Sal said. "You'll win this. Don't you always, Paul?"

Sal had the utmost confidence, not only in Paul, but in himself. He considered his high confidence level an asset to his job. Other people were not as sure about his conclusion.

Ahh, they're just jealous.

He picked up his notes of his hospital interview with Damien's girlfriend, Marsha Pickens, and began to read.

"Hey, Paul. There's more here than even I first thought. According to Agnossi's girlfriend, there was quite a bit of animosity between Kysen and Agnossi. They were each being considered for the same promotion. He had hinted he suspected our church-guy was 'cooking the books' with his financial report. So what do you think about that deacon now?"

Sal paused to read more.

"Oh . . . ho . . . ho, get a load of this! A big area of friction had to do with their religion versus science discussions. Seems to me Agnossi was about to prove the professor wrong about God creatin' the universe. That seems like a pretty good motive for foul play, don't you think?

"These creationists can get pretty fierce 'bout protecting their religious ideas. Surprises me the professor even believed that way, but maybe his plan was to mess up the experiment all along. Then things got out of control."

"I don't care about their beliefs. I certainly don't want to get sidetracked over that issue. A crime was committed and we need to focus on that. Get me some physical evidence when you go over the lab: security video, blood samples, DNA, something! Or you'll be out of a job," said Paul.

He took the report from his detective's hand and tossed it on his desk.

"No problem," replied Sal. "First thing tomorrow after I stop for some brain food."

"Doughnuts aren't brain food. Fish is brain food."

Paul was about to add something about Sal's need for fewer calories but decided against it.

This guy really needs to lose some weight.

Paul felt disgust as he noticed his lead officer suck in his breath to button his jacket.

"Yeah, but fish for breakfast?" Sal grimaced. "Come on."

"Whatever, just hurry," Paul said as he pushed Sal out of his office.

He shut the door and went back to his desk. He noticed the paper where he had scribbled the name of Ted's lawyer. He read the name and smiled. He knew he had no trouble keeping this man in jail until he got the evidence he needed for a murder charge.

CHAPTER 18
BLACK HOLE

The ringing was so loud, it hurt Gene's ears. He saw prisoners in blue jumpsuits run past him. Smoke was everywhere.

He heard someone yell, "Get that!"

What?

He looked and saw only smoke. He jumped when something hit him. It was soft.

"A pillow?" said Gene as he woke up.

"Get the phone, Gene," grumbled his mother.

It had only been a dream. Yet by the time Gene answered the telephone with a sleepy "yeah," the caller had already hung up.

Gene rubbed his face with his hands and shook his head.

Man, I'm hungry.

He looked at the clock, which read 7:00 P.M. He had slept all day; apparently, so had his mother and Sophie. No wonder he was hungry.

He got up and stumbled into the kitchen. He made some tea with two tea bags. He always did this when he had trouble waking up. He had tried coffee once but found it utterly disgusting. He did not understand how his parents drank the stuff.

He put his cup in the microwave and set the timer for one minute. Then he went to grab some more oatmeal cookies but realized he had already finished them off. Finding nothing else to snack on in the cupboard, he went to the refrigerator.

"Mm, spaghetti," he said.

It was still in the pan, so he took it out and turned the stove on. The microwave beeped. He took his tea out and put milk and three teaspoons of sugar in it.

"Gag! It's a wonder you don't have diabetes with all that sugar," grumbled Sophie. "Who was on the phone?"

"I dunno; they hung up."

"Didn't they leave a message?"

"I didn't check."

Sophie moved to the telephone and pushed the button to retrieve a message. Realizing it was not for her, she handed the telephone to Gene.

"It's always for you. I don't know why I bother," she said with a sigh.

Gene took the telephone and listened to the message: "Hey, Gene, this is Kaleb. Where were you, dude? We were supposed to meet at the mall, or did you forget? Call me, but not at this number. I should be back home in a couple hours. Dude, you missed all the excitement!"

"Oh, no!" said Gene.

He hit his forehead with the palm of his hand and slid it down over his face.

I was supposed to meet Kaleb!

Sophie asked, "What's wrong now?"

At this, their mother was up and wide awake.

"Who's that? Is it your dad? What's going on?"

"It's nothing!" Gene yelled.

He tried to assure both women the world was still going on as normal—at least for them. For him, it had just sunk into the biggest black hole ever.

CHAPTER 19
JAIL CELL

Ted was cold. He curled up on the mattress and tried to warm himself with a thin blanket. He wanted to know how his family was, but the telephone in the cell was not working. He did not have anything to write with or on. It was just as well since he was unable to explain anything to his family.

He still tried to process the events of the night. He could not fathom what had happened after he left the lab.

And this . . . Why all the drama?

Ted wanted out of his cell. He had been too stunned to protest anything the police had done and was still in disbelief. He was actually in jail, and worse, he was not even sure why. The police had asked a few questions about the night at the lab. They seemed harmless enough, so he had answered them.

Surely this is some catastrophic mistake. I'll be out soon.

He had to get out because his family needed him. When he did get out, he had some questions such as why he had not been read his rights. He decided he should probably sleep but found it hard to believe anyone could sleep on the inch-thick mattress with duct tape holding it together. Also, it was cold, and the thin blanket was not enough, despite being wool.

This whole thing was so insulting and humiliating, especially when they made him remove his watch and wedding ring. He had never had the ring off in the eighteen years since his young wife had nervously placed it on his finger.

How's she handling this? How's Sophie . . . and Gene?

He had not seen exactly what had happened with his son. He had only heard the screaming. It was distressing for Ted to hear his son, although almost a man, scream for him and not be able to help; it made him feel so powerless.

God, why? What's going on? I confess, Lord, this event has me worried. I'm trying to stay calm, but it's so hard when I don't know what's really going on—with me or my family. God, help me and watch over my family.

When it had finally sunk in that he was going to spend that night or more in jail, Ted found himself worrying about a dozen details. He had reassured himself there was nothing more he was able to do, so he needed to trust God. However, he had to keep reminding himself of that.

Ted usually was able to take things in stride.

But this . . . this is too much. What do the police think I've done . . . and why do they have to resort to such extreme measures? Just a few questions can clear things up. They haven't even told me anything of substance yet. They asked about things at the lab . . . Something must've happened there. I must've broken some environmental protection act.

He tried unsuccessfully to make light of his situation. Ted thought about work and all his problems with his boss.

Agnossi must've accused me of something, but what?

Then he remembered their last conversation about the fiscal reports. Ted's eyes widened. He needed to talk to his family.

CHAPTER 20

CRIME SCENE

The sun coming through the narrow window woke Darwin up. He had used his coat for a pillow and was rather stiff. He had forgotten where he was. Last night's dreams had been crazy, yet so realistic. He found himself wondering if he was able to recreate the machine he had seen in his dreams and for what in the world it was possibly used.

The light coming from it had been so bright. The noise was strange.

How can I dream up something I've never seen or a sound I've never heard? Alas, it was only a dream.

As Darwin stood, he felt rather dizzy. He ran his hand through his hair and felt liquid. When he brought his hand into focus, he realized he was bleeding. It had been bleeding, and a scab had formed, yet having been disturbed, it was leaking more blood.

How the devil did I do this?

He looked for a chair to sit on, only to realize he was in a small room filled with strange items. He tried to rub his eyes.

"Ouch! What the devil?"

He opened the door and looked out. There it was.

That contraption!

It was quiet, but it was definitely the machine from his dreams.

84

But, wait, if I'm not dreaming now, this means what happened last night was real. And that screaming man, where is he?

He did not know whether to be spooked or awed. His investigative mind had to explore.

He moved the yellow ribbons around the machine and stared in awe. He reached out and touched it and it was real. As he moved around the machine, he heard distant voices coming from outside. He moved to the windows and looked out.

Oh my! A lot of young people, but what strange clothes they're wearing.

Some were riding bicycles strangely put together, and some were riding bicycles that seemed to propel themselves, but what an awful noise they made. Darwin thought he had to be dreaming.

This just can't be real.

As he turned from the window to take another look at that contraption, he knocked several items off a shelf. He picked them up to return them to the shelf. Before he could make sense of anything he saw, he heard heavy footsteps come toward him. Men were conversing in an angry tone.

"If I get my hands on that guy again . . ." one of the men said.

This remark immediately registered to Darwin as a man he did not wish to encounter. He hurried back into the closet he had spent the night in, looking for a place to hide.

Just as he found a spot to hide, he heard the door open. He strained his ears to hear how many men were there.

Two . . . no, three.

They were talking about breakfast and something called Krispy Kreme. He was not sure what that was, but for the first time, he realized he was quite hungry. Then the door to his closet opened and he froze.

"Hey, John, I'm going to put my breakfast in here so I don't contaminate the scene."

"If you can call doughnuts and coffee a breakfast, Sal," replied the other man.

"Hey, this is brain food. I been eating this for breakfast for years, and ain't nobody solved as many crimes as me."

"Well, since this crime won't take any brains to solve, I won't argue with you," John replied. "Let's hurry up and get the evidence. I've got tons of paperwork to do and I want to leave the office early today. My kid's got a ball game."

John Hill, a fifteen-year veteran of the police force, loved his job and was a stickler for details. However, he also loved his children and hated when his job interfered with their time together.

Darwin's stomach growled.

"Hey, John, you sound hungry. Sure you don't want some brain food, seein' as you can use some," Sal chuckled.

"Huh? No thanks. I don't want to deprive you of any brain power, seeing as you still haven't fully evolved from your Neanderthal relatives," he said and laughed.

"I just offered you a doughnut, and this is the thanks I get? Sheesh."

Just then a third voice spoke, "Hey, detective, need you on the phone ASAP."

Both men immediately left the room.

As Darwin began to breathe again, he noticed the doughnuts left on the counter. They smelled good and he was not able to resist. He took one and pinched a small piece off and popped it into his mouth. It was delightful. He took another, and then another. He was so hungry he ate both doughnuts and the strange-tasting tea without even considering his manners.

Then another thought entered his mind. They had been talking about a crime and looking for "that man."

Is it me?

Given the blood on his hands and what he had seen on the floor, he was afraid to find out. Additionally, given the strangeness of the place and unfamiliarity of everything, he felt it best to remain hidden.

However, he was not used to sitting still and his muscles cramped. He decided to try to look around again, but as he stood to let himself out of his hideaway, he felt a familiar nausea and vertigo. He had to sit down again. As soon as it passed, he got up slowly and peeked outside the closet. No one was present, so he ventured out.

That marvelous machine was still there. He wondered if there might be some sort of instruction book. At least he may know if he was still in England if he found books written in English. It did not take long to find some.

Yes!

Most of the books were, indeed, of a scientific nature, but unlike any he had come across before. The binding was so perfect and the pages, so white.

As he looked through the titles, he came across a few books that actually had his name in the title! Those he had to read, but before he found a comfortable place to read, he heard footsteps. Not wanting another encounter, he quickly grabbed several books and rushed back into his little closet. He tried not to make any sound as he slid inside and closed the door.

CHAPTER 21
THE CONVERSATION

SUNDAY, MAY 24
2:10 PM

Gene picked up the telephone on his side of the glass window, as his mother finished saying good-bye to his father. He felt very strange, even a little afraid, to be in the visitation hall at the jail. It reminded him of his ordeal at the detention center—an ordeal he wanted to forget, even if he acted as though it did not bother him.

He took in all the sights and sounds around him: the crying baby, the preschooler screaming to talk to his daddy, and the frustrated mother telling her daughter, "daddy will be home soon," while tears streamed down her cheeks. She looked as if she had not slept much in the past few days.

At the far cubicle, an older lady with graying hair and no makeup told her son how ungrateful he was after all she had done for him. Her voice grew louder. The louder it got, the more curse words spewed forth.

"Gene. Gene, it's your turn," Sylvia's tearful voice interrupted his thoughts. "You haven't much time."

Gene put the telephone up to his ear.

"I was afraid you might not be able to come," his father said through the telephone receiver. "I was also afraid you didn't want to come, Gene. How are you holding up?"

They were in a small room with several telephone cubicles. The inmates sat on one side, most looking like they had just woken up. They were all in different-colored jumpsuits. Most were in green, but some were in tan or yellow.

Visitors were on the other side, separated by glass. The telephones were the only way they were able to talk to each other. Gene felt uneasy. There was no privacy and he did not want to show any emotion.

"There's no way I wasn't going to come, Dad. I mean, it's hard to see you like this, but I had to see how you're doing. I'm fine," replied Gene.

"Gene, I just found out what they're charging me with. I can assure you it's all false. There's no truth to these charges."

"I know, Dad."

"Your mom told me what they did to you. I didn't see anything, just heard shouts and thumps. Geeesh, what a nightmare! How are you holding up?"

"Okay," Gene said and then relieved their awkward silence. "How come you're wearing a different color than everyone else?"

"I'm special . . . considered a risk or violent, so I have to wear yellow. Green is the normal color. Tan means you're an inmate worker. You actually get out of your cell to do something."

More silence, and then Ted said, "I'm stunned by what they did to me and you too. I'm furious they treated you the way they did! Your mom informed me about stopping by the hospital. How are you feeling now?"

"It's okay, Dad. It added some excitement to my life. I'll get a little extra attention at school, but I'm more worried about you. Anything I can get for you? Anything I can do? Mom's handling all the legal stuff. I don't really know much about what's going on with that."

"Actually, you can. I've got so much research and reading to catch up on. That is, if I still have a job after all this. Can you ask your mom to pick up my research papers from my office? They're in my brown briefcase."

"Sure. I actually got some reading done for my science report. Did you know Haeckel's embryos are fakes? Yet they still have them in our science books as proof of our evolution!"

"Yes, pretty slimy of them, isn't it? That reminds me. Next to my briefcase are some books I picked out to help you on your report. How—"

Just then a voice came over the telephone to announce, "Time's up."

Ted let out a sigh.

"Hang in there, Gene, and keep an eye on your mom and sister. Your mom's gonna need your help. Stay strong."

"Sure, Dad," Gene replied.

Gene wanted to slam the telephone down. It made him angry to see his father in yellow coveralls. It made him angry to know that they were charging him. It also made him angry that he had to go through what he did. He wanted to punch the wall, but he kept his anger to himself. His mother was watching him; he had to stay strong for her.

It had been a strange visit. Gene did not feel free to say what he wanted. His mother had warned him the telephone conversations might be recorded. There was so much he wanted to ask his father.

At first, he had wanted to ask what he had done last week that they needed to talk about. However, Gene forgot all about that when he saw him in that place with rough-looking inmates. Whatever had caused friction between them before no longer mattered.

CHAPTER 22
THE DECISION

That night, Gene tried to study. He still had his report to do. His teacher had given him extra time, but Gene did not think time was going to help.

Geesh, they tell us it took billions of years to evolve, yet they expect us to get a report about it done in a few days!

Gene thought about his visit with his father. Sylvia had tried to get the papers, but the police were not letting anyone in or out of the crime scene—definitely no evidence was allowed out of the lab.

His father had talked about his creation research quite a bit. As a matter of fact, he and Ted had argued about it last week. Up until this year, Gene had always agreed with his father's version of creation. It had not gone well when he told Ted his science teacher had presented some pretty convincing evidence that the earth was millions of years old.

When he confessed his thoughts that science had confirmed evolution to be true, his father lectured him off and on the whole day. Gene imagined what his father might have said if he had confessed his growing doubts God existed. After discovering that book at the hospital, Gene wanted to learn more.

It was hard for Gene to accept the young age his father believed the earth to be. That was his biggest concern. He wanted to believe, but that age thing bothered him. He had so many questions and wished he was able to look at those other books in that moment. It just was not right for his whole life to be a mess. He needed his father.

It just isn't fair!

Gene felt anger rise inside. It felt awful to feel so helpless.

Sometimes being a kid isn't as easy as grownups think it is. Being a teenager is even worse!

He was old enough to know what could go wrong but too young to do anything about it!

There's gotta be something I can do!

Then it hit him.

Why not get the papers and books myself? Why should I worry about getting into any more trouble?

He felt like he had been punished for simply reacting to the police invasion.

So why not go ahead and do something illegal? After all, it isn't like I'm killing somebody or stealing something. Who will know if I cross some stupid police line? So what if I'm not supposed to go inside the lab? I can't stand by and watch Dad go to prison when I can go to that lab, look for evidence, and get those books.

He'd given his teacher his topic and was stuck with it now. What he was about to do could help himself and his dad.

With the decision made and his anger still at full throttle, he started to call his friend C. M. but noticed the clock. It was 11:30 P.M.

How did it get so late so fast?

C. M. may not mind, but his stepfather might. C. M. said he was not a very patient or understanding person.

Better not risk getting him into trouble.

It was okay to risk his neck, but not someone else's. Besides, C. M. seemed to be rather standoffish lately.

Gene had tried to call him earlier that evening, but C. M. was out with friends.

I wonder who his new friends are. He certainly isn't hanging out with our group. He didn't even return my call about game night. That was something he never missed before.

Kaleb might be able to help. After all, he had a permit. However, it was too late to call him too. If only he had a cell phone, he might have called earlier. Sophie and his mother had the telephone tied up all day. Of course, his mother needed it to talk to lawyers.

At that moment, Gene resented not having a cell phone like the rest of the kids at school. His mother had said he could have one when he started to drive, but that did not help him at that moment. Unfortunately, Kaleb did not have a cell phone either, so it did not really matter.

"Aw man!" he said out loud.

He had just remembered he was supposed to have met Kaleb and Alexis at the mall earlier that day. That had been the backup plan if Saturday did not work out.

"Two days in a row. She's going to think I don't like her."

He got up to go call Kaleb despite the late hour, but when he went downstairs, he heard his mother talking on the telephone. She sounded as if she had been crying. He listened for a moment when he heard her mention his father's name.

". . . and this lawyer did nothing! He just let them get away with keeping Ted locked up for murder even though the victim is still alive! Can you believe that?" his mother asked.

"What? Oh, the last I heard he's still in a coma. As you can imagine, I'm not allowed to visit him."

She paused to listen.

"Uh-huh. Yes, I can use your help. If you know of any good lawyers I can get, let me know. I feel so stupid for hiring this guy. I should never have listened to . . ."

Dad's not getting out. This is sooo unfair.

Gene had to get to that lab, even if he had to drive himself in his father's car. Not wanting to disrupt his mother's conversation, he quietly retreated to his room.

He felt frustrated . . . really frustrated as he punched his pillow and then flopped on his bed. He lay there with his hands behind his head. He was not sure what bothered him more: that he had stood up Alexis or that his mother was upset and crying. He lay wishing he was older so he did not have to rely on someone else for a telephone or ride.

After a few moments of feeling sorry for himself, he decided to take matters into his hands.

I'll just go by myself.

He got up immediately to gather some stuff to take with him. He was so intent in his thoughts and trying to figure out what he needed, that he almost did not hear the soft knock as the door opened.

"Gene?" Sophie whispered. "Gene, you still up? I got an idea I want to tell you about—What are you all dressed in black for?"

She entered before he was able to shut the door or protest her barging into his room.

"You're going to get Dad's papers . . . I knew it! Wait a minute and I'll get my stuff!"

"No way," Gene whispered so loud it was hardly a whisper. "You can't come with me. I don't want you slowing me down or getting hurt."

"Oh, and just how are you going to get inside a locked office?" she asked.

"I'll figure out something."

"How about a key . . . like this key?" she taunted as she held up a small golden key.

"Where'd you get that from?"

"Never mind that. Since you don't want me to come . . . you know you probably shouldn't go either. It can be dangerous for you too, and . . . well, given your legal problems . . . well, I think Mom needs to know about this."

Gene let out an exasperated sigh. "You wouldn't! Why, I'll just—"

"You'll just what?" taunted Sophie.

Gene glared at his sister. He started to explain just what he wanted to do and then thought it better to have her help.

"Okay. You got me. We'll do this together, but I'm leaving in half an hour, and I'm not waiting!"

"No problem," replied Sophie with a triumphant smile. "So how are we going to get to the lab?"

CHAPTER 23
MEETING THE PAST

MONDAY, MAY 25
2:00 AM

"Shh," said Sophie.

She turned the key and heard it click. It seemed so loud in the quiet building; any noise seemed like a sonic boom.

"I didn't say anything," replied Gene.

He turned and looked at C. M., who just shrugged.

"Well, you are now!" retorted Sophie.

"I'll tell you what," said C. M. "You guys don't need me in here, but we can use a lookout. I'm going out by the stairway. It's close enough to warn you if anyone is coming. I can keep an eye on our ride and make sure they don't ditch us."

"Scared?" teased Gene.

"No. If anyone comes, I'd be the first caught. Duh."

"Yeah, you're right on both counts. I'm just glad you came by tonight when you did. I'm surprised my mom answered the door that late," Gene said. "Hey, you never did say why you came by."

"You kinda made it hard for me to get a word in. I was just gonna ask to crash at your place for the night. The guys wanted to go someplace and I couldn't go along. Good for you they liked the idea of helping you sneak in here. You'll have to retell your story as to why we're here. It didn't make any sense, but for you to do something like this is, well, interesting."

"Who are those guys anyway?" asked Gene.

"Just my older brother and his friend."

"Well, whatever, we kinda need to hurry. Are you coming or not?" whispered Sophie.

She turned the knob and opened the door. Gene followed, but C. M. stayed outside.

Gene knew Sophie had been at their father's office before, but not the inner part because no one was allowed in there. She had a plastic card she had borrowed from her father's jacket. As she swiped it, the green light glowed; she pushed the inner door open.

"Wow!" Sophie and Gene said in unison and turned on their flashlights.

Inside the room was a giant machine that looked like it might be a spaceship on an operating table. It was a large cylinder on a heavy table with tubes and wires, and all sorts of things going to and coming from the cylinder. There were also several caution signs stating "Danger—Experiment in Progress" and "Caution: PPD's are Required."

"What is a PPD?" asked Sophie.

"That stands for *personal protective device*. Stuff you wear to keep chemicals and junk off of you."

"Oh. Do you think we should have some on?"

"Nah, you just need it when the machine's on or when you're doing the experiment," Gene said and then added, "At least I hope so!"

The sound of a door opening broke the silence of the night. Sophie jumped. Gene felt adrenaline zing through his whole body.

"Was that a mouse? Tell me that was just a mouse," whispered Sophie.

"Sounded like an awfully big mouse," whispered Gene.

"Let's go," said Sophie, trying hard not to panic.

"You can go if you want, but not me. I came here to get some stuff for Dad, and I'm not gonna let him down. So if you want to let a little ole mouse stop you—"

Crash!

Gene and Sophie let out screams.

"Oh my gosh! Did you see that . . . him . . . her . . . it . . . whatever!"

The fear in Sophie's voice shot to panic. Sensing her fear actually helped Gene get rid of his. Boldly, he shone his light in the direction the sound had come from, and then his courage disappeared.

CHAPTER 24
ILLUMINATION

Darwin was growing weary of hiding and thought he should face his fears head on and see what, or who, was out there. He knew he was no longer in London, unless his colleagues were playing one huge prank on him, but they were too professional for that. He was not completely convinced he was fully awake. After all, everything was so different from only a day ago. A person does not simply wake up in another place.

That's impossible.

Darwin had another very unpleasant thought: *What if I've died and gone to the afterlife, but which way did I go?*

It must have been the wrong way. He surely did not see any angels playing lovely harps.

Preposterous.

He had quit believing in that concept years ago. He was a scientist—there was a logical explanation. He needed to get up and find out what had transpired. Right after his bout of nausea subsided.

Oh. I must cut back on the laudanum when I finally wake up, he thought with a moan. *If I ever wake up!*

The hunger he felt was real. The pastry he had eaten that morning had been delicious, and he wanted more. Hunger propelled him to leave his hiding place. He heard no more voices, so he opened the door.

There's that monstrous machine.

As he studied it, he felt more than knew the machine had something to do with his being where he was. Yet he had no clue about how it worked.

He was so engrossed in studying the machine he forgot about his hunger and almost did not hear the door open and the ensuing voices. He hurried back to his closet and covered himself with lab coats. The voices whispered but sounded young—one voice sounded as if it were female. He was unable to make out what they were saying. He had to get closer, but he also needed something with which to defend himself.

He stood to look around the dimly lit closet and bumped his head on something. It was some sort of canister with a handle on it. He lifted it. It felt heavy enough to do bodily harm if he must. Since he did not know where he was or who those people were, it was prudent to be ready for danger.

He opened the door as quietly as possible. Not seeing anyone, he cautiously stepped out and lifted the canister to the ready position. As he took another step, his foot caught on something, and without thinking, he yanked his foot to free it. Unfortunately for him, this motion caused everything above him to fall. He made a futile attempt to protect himself.

Crash!

He heard screams and froze for a second. He frantically searched for a place to hide. Quickly, he spotted a recess in the shadows under a counter and ducked in just before the door opened to the room he was in.

A light shone into the room, but it was not the bright glow of candlelight or a lantern. It was brighter, yet small and directed. It lit everything pointed at. Darwin tried to squeeze into his hole even farther; not only because he did not want to be seen, but also because he did not know if the light might do more than just illuminate what it touched.

The sound of footsteps closed in on him. He looked for an escape from the room. All he saw was the corner of the recess he thought he would be able to get behind if the footsteps got too close. However, he was not quick enough. The light shone directly at him and blinded him.

△ △ △

Gene thought he saw someone, but it was just an old overcoat. His hand shook as he moved the beam around.

Crash!

"Sophie! What did you do?" asked Gene in a loud, angry whisper.

"Me! What did *you* do?" replied Sophie with equal anger.

"If it wasn't me and it wasn't you, then—"

Before Gene could finish his statement, a hissing sound, and white foam covered his face, and then Sophie's. Both of them let out screams and dropped their flashlights as they tried to cover their faces and back away from the foam. They tripped over each other and landed with a heavy thud on the floor—first Gene, and then Sophie. They let out grunts of pain as they stared into the shadowy face of a man with long, unruly hair wearing a dark overcoat

CHAPTER 25
TIME TRAVELER

That night was not going well for Darwin. As he tried to get around the corner, he knocked over a long pole. When he did, he stumbled and dropped the canister. It landed on the floor. As the handle touched the floor, out came a white substance that made what seemed a thunderous hiss. He tried to grab it but noticed the intruders being covered with white foam and letting out shrieks of fright and surprise.

Darwin started to bolt from the room but noticed it was only a pair of youth.

A young lad and girl.

He stopped. At first, he was puzzled, and then he wanted to make sure he had not done them any harm. As he started to help the girl stand, she let out a yell.

⚗ ⚗ ⚗

"Don't hurt me, mister! Please don't hurt me!" squeaked Sophie.

"Don't worry. I won't hurt you. What are you doing here?" asked Darwin with the tone of a scolding parent.

"What am *I* doing here? What are *you* doing here?" asked Sophie.

"Yeah. What are you doing here? This place is closed. There's a police *Do Not Cross* tape all around the room," said Gene.

His voice had more bravado than he felt.

Then he added to Sophie, "Get off of me!"

They both stood and grabbed their flashlights. The character their lights illuminated looked like an actor from a nineteenth-century play, with a long overcoat and high-collared white shirt. He was bald on top of his head but had long, bushy hair on the sides and a very long, gray beard.

"Why are you dressed like that?" inquired Sophie. "Surely play practice is over at this time of night."

"If no one is supposed to be in here, then might I ask what you two are doing? You don't look old enough to be out at this time of night without chaperones . . . and how else would a gentleman be dressed? It's you two who are dressed in funny attire," replied Darwin. "I'm Darwin. What are your names?"

"I'm Gene and this is my sister, Sophie," replied Gene with hesitation.

He was not sure he should have answered that question, but the guy seemed harmless, despite his weird appearance. Gene felt a sudden tingling of his nerves.

What if this is the real killer?

"This is my dad's laboratory; we came here to get his research papers," added Sophie.

"Shh!" hissed Gene.

"Oh, so this is a laboratory . . . and what's that mechanism? What kind of research do you do? I myself am a botanist and apprentice geologist. I'd be fascinated to learn more about your project and methods. Can I meet your father?" Darwin eagerly asked.

"Well, that won't be easy. Were you supposed to be in on the research? Do you know what happened here last night? Did you see anything?" asked Gene.

He wondered whether or not the guy in front of him was mentally stable.

"Well, I know how strange this is going to seem, but quite frankly, I don't know how I arrived here. One minute I was looking for my coat

. . . and . . . and then I'm here. There were bright lights shooting out from this contraption," said Darwin as he pointed to it.

"A man with fuzzy hair was standing over there by the machine. The noise was unbearable and I felt very queasy. I was trying to keep from falling when I noticed the man by the machine fell. As he did, everything on the table next to him fell as well. There were several glass beakers and all sorts of chemicals. I rushed over to help him.

"There was a gash on his head, and the chemicals were pouring all over him. So I removed the beakers and tried to look for a rag to mop up things with. It was obvious the chemicals were seeping into his body through the skin. Since my father is a doctor and I've attended patients with him, I felt it necessary to act quickly.

"I spied a scalpel and bent to make a slice on his arm to let out the toxic substances in his blood. As I made the first cut, he screamed and shouted at me to get away. He was so maniacal in his screams, it caused me to panic . . . and well, I started to run, but the first door I opened was that closet . . . and still feeling queasy . . . well, I hid."

Darwin inhaled and slowly released his breath as if trying to calm himself.

Gene stared, not sure if he should believe this story. His nerves were on edge, making it difficult to size up the man. Apparently, he had witnessed what happened, or he was the real criminal.

Should I trust this guy?

"So you witnessed what happened? We got to get you to the police so you can tell them this. Did you see any other people?" asked Sophie. "Oh, this has got to be good news for Dad, Gene!"

"Wait, Soph. Mr. Darwin, why did you want to cut him to let out blood?" asked Gene cautiously. "Doctors haven't done that since the 1800s."

"That's the standard and best practice of this day, I'll have you know," Darwin replied defensively.

"Which century are you from?" asked Gene with sarcasm.

He was beginning to wonder if he and Sophie might be in danger. *This guy might be crazy.*

"Well, it was 1871 when I woke up yesterday morning. Quite frankly, the past day has me wondering that same thing."

"You're kidding me, right? You off your meds?"

"Meds?"

"Yeah, you know: Valium, lithium, OxyContin?"

"I don't know what those are. I just take a little laudanum now and then for my nervous stomach."

"What's your full name?" Gene asked with suspicion.

"Charles Darwin. Scientist. Botanist. Writer. What's your full name?"

"You mean *the* Charles Darwin?" Gene asked with a laugh. "Yeah, right. He's been dead for over a century!"

"I'll have you know I'm quite alive. Although sometimes I must confess I wish it were not so when my health is in a detrimental state. I do feel it may suffer quite adversely from all this. What is today's date?"

"May 24th, actually 25th now, 2009."

They all looked at each other skeptically. Neither Darwin nor Gene nor Sophie believed what was apparently going on.

Can this man be the genuine Charles Darwin from history? But time travel isn't possible, or is it?

CHAPTER 26
TED'S DECISION

MONDAY, MAY 25
3:02 AM

Ted woke up to a dimly lit room. His head was still a bit fuzzy, but one attempt to turn over and get comfortable reminded him where he was. His back ached. Never had he had trouble with back pain before, but with a thin foam mattress atop an unbending steel frame, it was no wonder. Unable to sleep, he sat up on his bunk, but it was no use getting up.

It's forbidden—everything's forbidden.

It was even forbidden for Sylvia to retrieve his papers from the lab. He had really hoped to get them to do something productive while he waited for the lawyer to straighten things out. He wondered how the kids and Sylvia were doing. He felt a need to talk to them, but that was not going to happen anytime soon. He had just found out that day his bail had been denied.

Well, he was able to write letters since he finally had some paper and a little pencil. He decided to write to Gene first. He knew his son was struggling with a science report on evolution and creation. He had so much to tell him because he had been looking for books to help Gene understand why it was so important to have the correct view of creation.

What you believe about this issue affects your actions.

As he began to write the titles of the books he wanted Gene to read, he was amused. One was entitled *Darwin on Trial*. It dawned on him how there might be parallels to trying the evidence for evolution and his innocence.

He wrote out his thoughts. Then he rewrote his thoughts as if he were making a case for creation. He finished the letter to Gene, wrote to Sophie and Sylvia, and was still wide awake. He liked to make good use of his time. In jail, he only worried. He did not like to call it worrying, but it was.

He had only spent three full days in jail, but it felt as if a month had passed. Time passed slower than a sleepy slug. He wished he were able to speed up time until he was back home, sleeping on a comfortable bed. Then the thought he had tried to keep in the back of his mind came forward with the force of a tornado.

What if I never get out of this place?

Tears began to fall . . . slowly at first and then in uncontrollable bursts. His body trembled as he tried to be quiet. His nose began to run, so he put his pillow over his face to quiet his sobs and sniffles.

Why, God? Why is this happening?

Anger started to take over the utter sadness and hopelessness he had been feeling. He felt or sensed a voice telling him to pray, to tell God how he felt.

Isn't this what a Christian is supposed to do?

He did not want to pray, but he found himself doing it anyway. At first, he poured out all his feelings to God, even the angry ones. Then he took out his Bible, but he really did not feel like reading it. He wanted to keep an upbeat outlook, but with the way his case was going and the trouble his wife and kids were having, he needed to read his Bible.

He needed to get over his anger. He had been able to hold his emotions in check so far, but he did not know how much longer he was able to take his current situation. If only someone talked with him.

He was sure he could clear it up and then make them pay for what they had done to his son.

He sat there for a moment, unable to open the book which had once brought him so much joy. Then he remembered the verse that told him to "rejoice in all things."

Yeah, right. God, if You're there, talk to me, 'cause I can't quit feeling angry.

He forced himself to open his Bible and turn to the Book of Psalms.

Praise . . . That's the last thing I feel like doing.

He read anyway. It was strange how after only a couple of chapters, a feeling of peace descended upon him. After a few more chapters, tears streamed down his cheeks. He started to wipe them away with the wool blanket but quickly discovered it was not a good idea. So he chuckled and let the tears flow. It felt so good, so cleansing.

Lord, I know now You have a sense of humor. I've felt so overwhelmed and tired, wanting rest. God, I wanted a rest . . . not to be arrested.

Then after a moment longer he continued to pray, *Lord, I don't know why I'm here, why I have to go through this, or why Sylvia and the kids have to go through this, but, Lord, I surrender my will to Yours. There's obviously nothing I can do, and I now see that. What do You want me to learn from this?*

I can see so many ways I've failed You and my family, especially my son. I can see I've been so hard on him, taking a lot of my frustrations at work out on him because I don't want to see him end up like some of those students. I pray for my wife and kids. Keep them safe and give them wisdom and success in all they do. Amen.

As soon as he began to pray, a pleasant sensation overwhelmed him. It was as if he was able to feel the actual presence of God in his jail cell. Strange, he felt freer locked up than on the outs—slang he had picked up from the other inmates. Even in jail he felt the presence of God—more than in church the last time he went. Feeling rested, he lay on the mattress and fell asleep.

CHAPTER 27

IS IT REALLY YOU?

"So you're Charles Darwin?" Gene asked one more time.

He was still unable to believe the man before him was who he said. The very man he had been reading about and who he was about to write a report on.

He's caused me so much turmoil because of that stupid report.

Gene did not know what else to say. He had trouble believing this encounter.

"Cool!" said Sophie, never at a loss for words. "Hey, Gene, now you won't even have to read all those books sitting on your desk at home! You get to talk to the author . . . Wow!"

Gene sneered at his sister.

How can she just accept what this stranger is saying? Of course, if he is who he says . . . well . . . won't that be . . .

Gene was unable to think of the word. He had just learned it in his English class.

What's that fancy word that means "lucky"? Oh, yeah, serendipitous— *what luck!*

"That'd be serendipitous, to be sure, but, Sophie, you don't really believe this guy, do you?"

"Don't you remember Dad telling us about the possibility of time travel? Maybe this machine somehow acted like a time transporter?"

"You mean like a flux capacitor for a DeLorean?" mocked Gene.

"I don't know, but maybe."

Gene let out a sigh.

"Excuse me, I don't know anything about time travel, but, yes, I'm Charles Darwin. And you still haven't told me what you children are doing out in the middle of the night!"

Darwin put down the fire extinguisher, wiped off his jacket with his hands, and said, "I hope I didn't hurt you children with that white foam. I do apologize."

"No, we're fine. You just scared the life out of me! I thought you were gonna kill us or something. Are you okay?" asked Sophie.

Gene looked warily at his sister and the man who claimed to be Darwin.

"There was a crime here last night. Can't you see all the police tape?" asked Gene. "A man was attacked and almost killed. You don't know anything about that, do you?"

"Yeah, the guy my dad works for was assaulted, and the police think my dad did it, but we know he didn't, and we're gonna prove it!" insisted Sophie, ignoring her brother's looks.

"Sophie, shut up!" Gene demanded in a low, serious voice.

He still was not too sure about the harmlessness of the stranger.

"Hey," said Sophie, "you must've seen what happened. That guy you saw and tried to help, what did he look like?"

"The man who fell ill last night? I can't quite remember. Everything happened so quickly, and quite honestly, I wasn't sure whether I was dreaming or not! Apparently, I frightened him as much as he frightened me when I suddenly found myself in this strange place. I tried to help him. He fainted."

"Shush!" hissed Gene. "I hear noises!"

"Oh my gosh, we're gonna be in big trouble!" Sophie cried out. "We need to hide!"

"Quick, in the closet!" whispered Darwin.

He caught the fear in the kid's voices and did not want any more stressful encounters. Sophie followed him, but Gene grabbed her arm. Sophie turned and looked pleadingly at Gene.

"If the night watchman catches us, we'll all be in trouble, especially you!"

Gene thought for a moment. *Crazy guy or night watchman: which is worse? This guy seemed harmless enough.*

The click of a doorknob turning propelled Gene into action. They all tumbled into the closet.

No one said a word. Even their breathing was hushed. Sure enough, there were footsteps. They saw the beam of a flashlight filter under the door. They heard the doorknob rattle, but it did not open.

Silence.

Then to everyone's relief, the footsteps continued down the hall.

"Whew, that was close!" whispered Sophie.

"That's for sure," Gene agreed. "We need to get out of here and quick, but I gotta find those books Dad wanted me to get. Soph, come on, we need to take one quick look around."

"But what about Mr. Darwin?"

"What about him?"

"Yes, what about me?" interjected Darwin.

"We can't leave him here! Besides, he can answer a lot of questions about what really happened."

Sophie gave Gene a pleading look.

"After overhearing Mom and the lawyer talk, I don't think anyone will believe us or that this is the real Charles Darwin. Besides, I don't trust the cops. Just the way they talked to everyone, it seemed they had their minds made up."

"We gotta get some proof before we tell anybody what we know," explained Sophie.

"Good point, but where will we take him?" asked Gene sarcastically.

"To our house, of course. We have the den that no one ever uses. He can stay there."

"We can't do that! What will Mom say?"

"Nothing, if we don't tell her. Besides, she has enough to worry about."

"You sure didn't listen to the 'do not talk to strangers' talk, let alone the 'do not take strangers home with you' talk," Gene complained.

He felt himself agreeing with his sister. Admittedly, he did have a lot of questions for Darwin.

"Okay. What do you say, Mr. Darwin—do you want to come with us?"

"Yes. It'll be nice to sleep on a real bed, but I do think we should make sure it's okay with your mother first," replied Darwin.

"It's too late to ask Mom tonight, and she'd freak out if she knew we were here!" Gene said.

"You can say that again!" replied Sophie. "Hey, he can sleep on the patio. It's not really *in* the house and the cushions are really soft. It'll be a lot better than here. It's nice enough outside."

"That'll work," Gene agreed and then added as he faced Darwin, "and that way you can get cleaned up while she's at work so you don't look like a homeless person off the streets."

"Ahh, how nice it'll be to heat up some water on the fire for a bath," Darwin mused with a sigh.

"Oh, you don't have to heat up water on the fire. You just turn on the hot water, silly," Sophie teased.

"Don't forget, he doesn't know what that is. Man, have we got a lot to show you. A lot has changed in the past century and a half!" said Gene.

Despite his doubts, Gene hoped the guy really was who he said.

"Let's go then," insisted Sophie. "The longer we're here, the more chances we have of getting caught. I'm starting to get creeped out!"

"Wait!" whispered Gene.

"What is it?" hissed Sophie. She was beginning to feel spooked.

"We haven't found the papers we came here to get! Soph, check the desk. I'll check the lab. Mr. Darwin, check the closet. We're looking for a brown briefcase and a blue Trapper."

Noticing the confused look on Darwin's face, Gene continued, "Uh, er, I mean a blue notebook and some books about evolution and creation."

"You mean my theory got accepted!" exclaimed Darwin. "Have they found the missing intermediary morphologic fossils?"

"Well—"

"Wait," interjected Darwin.

He ran into the closet and ruffled through the tumble of items on the floor.

"Here they are!"

Darwin held up three books, looking quite pleased. He no longer looked like an old man as he excitedly pointed to one of the books.

"Look! This one has my name in the title: *The Theory of Evolution and Darwin's Black Box*! Over one hundred and fifty years and my theory still stands! What was in my black box? I thought my papers were stored in a brown trunk."

Sophie started to giggle but covered her mouth and looked at Gene.

"I dunno," answered Gene. "That's what I was going to find out. It's my dad's book. He said it'll help me do my report. Do you know, Soph?"

"We can talk about it later, in the comfort of our home. Now that we've got everything, we can go. Hurry!" Sophie insisted.

She picked up the blue Trapper with all her dad's notes and put them in his briefcase.

"This is it, right?" she asked Gene.

"Looks like it. Quick, put that stuff back where it was before we came in, and let's get out of here. We don't want more trouble for getting caught messing up a crime scene!"

The three of them carefully entered the hallway and closed the door behind them. Gene looked all around. He let out a low whistle to see if his friend answered.

"Where's C. M.?"

CHAPTER 28
WHAT NOW?

3:29 AM

"What do we do now?" asked Sophie as panic rose in her voice.

"Let's get outside. Maybe he's waiting by the car," said Gene.

They hurried to get outside and went to the spot where their ride had dropped them off. There was no sign of C. M. There was no ride either.

"Oh my gosh!" said Sophie. "What do we do now?"

"Stay cool," said Gene, stifling his panic. "C. M. may just be hiding. We wait for him."

"What if he doesn't show up?"

"Just wait a few minutes."

Thirty minutes later, C. M. still had not shown up. Gene tried to hide the unease building up inside him that they had been abandoned.

"Have we waited long enough?" asked Sophie. "I say we've been ditched and we need to find a way back, and quick!"

Gene did not want to admit he had been ditched, but he knew Sophie was right. They had to get moving.

But how . . . Walk?

Gene estimated it should take them three or four hours to walk home—making an arrival time around 7:00 A.M.

Mom will definitely be up by then. She'll absolutely freak out if she finds our rooms empty.

"Let's get walking," he said with a sigh.

115

He shook Darwin, who had fallen asleep.

How can the man sleep sitting up?

"Huh . . . What . . . What happened? You'll never believe the dream I had!"

Darwin rubbed his face with his hands. He opened his eyes and saw Gene. Disappointment registered in his face.

"I'm not dreaming, am I?"

"No, and we've got lots of walking to do. We have to get a move on it."

They had only been walking about five minutes when they heard a loud clapping noise.

"A horse and buggy!" yelled Darwin. "We can just take a taxi. Quick, do you children have any money? How much do these things cost these days? I think I might have a few coins in my pocket."

He began to pat his pockets to feel for any coins.

"That's not a taxi," said Gene. "Not even close. We can't get a ride from them."

"Why not?" interrupted Sophie.

She ran toward the Amish buggy. She stepped out into the street and waved the buggy down.

"Can we help ye?" asked a young bearded man wearing a round hat.

"We need a ride to our house. Can you fit the three of us in there? We'll pay, of course," said Sophie.

"Well, I don't think I've ever given an English person a ride home. Why not? We're supposed to help those in need, and ye looks in need. Hop in."

Gene climbed in the front seat to give the driver directions while Sophie and Darwin got in the back next to another younger man. He did not look much older than Gene, but Sophie did not know what to say when he gave her a big grin. Sophie smiled back and then looked away.

The driver of the buggy laughed and said, "Don't mind Joshua. He, uh, just had a little too much fun with his English friends. My name is Samuel. What be your names?"

Gene introduced everyone and gave Samuel directions to his house. Darwin broke the silence.

"I'm English too. Are you Irish or Scottish?"

The driver looked at him strangely.

"What did I say wrong?" he whispered to Sophie.

"We're all English to them. They're Amish," answered Sophie.

"Actually, we're German . . . Can trace our line back to 1620!" Samuel said.

CHAPTER 29
COVERT OPERATION

6:23 AM

Gene sneaked in the back door, careful not to make any noise. Fortunately, it was close enough to his normal time to get up, so if he woke his mother, he would be able to explain he was doing laundry he had forgotten to do the previous day. Sophie followed, shushing Darwin and waving him inside. Gene waited for them to enter before he turned on the light and started for his room. He tripped over Darwin, who had suddenly stopped.

"How did you do that?" he asked, amazed.

"Do what?" hissed Gene.

He was still a little sore and stiff from that long ride in the Amish buggy. He had a new appreciation for cars and comfortable seats.

"Turn on the light without a fire starter?" Darwin replied.

Gene hesitated a moment and gave him a quizzical look. Then he pointed to the switch.

"Duh!"

Then it dawned on him that Darwin was from the nineteenth century and many things had changed.

"I mean, we now have a lot more inventions since your time. You've traveled almost a hundred and fifty years into the future. We have tons of things to show you," said Gene enthusiastically.

"Wow, this is gonna be sweet!" added Sophie.

"Well, first, may I beg your servant to draw me a bath?" asked Darwin.

"Sorry. We don't have any servants. We do it all ourselves. I could *draw* you a bath, but I'm not a good artist. How about you take a shower instead?"

Gene was unable to resist saying something smart. Sophie rolled her eyes.

"Just show him to the bathroom! Quick, before Mom wakes up. Explain how things work . . . You know, maybe we should wait until Mom leaves for work. I really don't think she'll be too happy if we surprise her with a stranger in her house this early in the morning. We need to decide how to get out of school today. Do you think Mom will suspect anything if we both pretend to be sick?" asked Sophie.

"I was thinking about that on the way home. I think we can pull it off. We can say it was cafeteria food or something like that," Gene suggested.

"*That*, she'll believe. I was complaining about the food yesterday," she said.

So Gene took Darwin to show him a twenty-first-century bathroom. He explained how to flush a toilet and turn on the shower. Darwin was fascinated and wanted to turn the shower and faucets on and off. The toilet really fascinated him. He laughed like a kid.

Darwin kept saying, "Marvelous! Imagine that!"

Gene backed out of the bathroom and closed the door. He listened to ensure Darwin did not have any problems.

"Who's in the shower if both of you are in the hall?" asked Sylvia.

Gene and Sophie turned to their mother with startled expressions. Gene dropped Darwin's coat, which he had taken to run it through the washer and dryer. Sophie bent over.

"Oh, my stomach . . . I think I'm going to throw up again!"

"What's the matter, Sophie?" Sylvia asked.

She went to Sophie and put her arm on her daughter's shoulder.

"Gene, what's that you just dropped on the floor?"

"Oh, that's a prop from play practice," Sophie said before Gene answered.

She gave her brother a look to get in his room and then faked another stomach pain.

"I think I ate something bad at school yesterday. I'm not feeling well!"

Gene got the message and picked up the coat. He opened and closed the bathroom door as if he went back inside but tiptoed to his room before his mother saw him.

"Oh, ooh!" Sophie continued her moans. "Mom, I feel awful. Do I have to go to school?"

"Go back to your room and I'll make you some herbal tea. If you're not feeling better by the time I get ready, I won't make you go to school."

Sylvia turned, knocked on the bathroom door, and yelled, "Hurry up in there and don't use up all the hot water!"

She did not expect an answer, let alone the deep baritone, "As you wish," with a slight British accent. She turned and gave Sophie a puzzled look.

Sophie shrugged and said, "Must be that voice-change thing, combined with helping me too much with play rehearsal."

Sylvia nodded and said, "Uh-huh."

She shook her head and rubbed her face and then headed to the kitchen to make the tea.

Sophie heard her say, "I think I'm really losing my mind."

Sophie waved to her brother to get Darwin.

"The coast is clear!"

Gene tiptoed back to the bathroom, pushed the door ajar, and whispered as loud as possible, "Hurry, Mr. Darwin . . . Get done! My mom is up! You gotta get out of the house before she sees you!"

He threw a robe and towels into the bathroom and shut the door. Fortunately, he remembered to keep one. He heard his mother's hurried footsteps and threw the towel over his head as if he had just come out of the shower.

"Gene, is that you? Come here and get this tea for your sister so I can get my shower."

"Oh, ooh!" moaned Gene. "Hey, Mom, I musta ate the same thing as Sophie. I'm not feeling too well either. You might want to wait before you use the bathroom."

He held his hands on his stomach and peered up from under his towel to see if his mother was buying his act.

"Not you too! I'll make some more tea."

She went back to the kitchen. Gene saw the bathroom door open slowly.

"Is it safe to come out now?"

Gene waved Darwin into the hall closet, which had just enough room for him to squeeze into. Then Gene hurried into the bathroom to ensure there was no evidence of Darwin having been in there.

CHAPTER 30
PLAYING HOOKY

Gene and Sophie managed to get Sylvia to let them stay home from school without suspecting a thing, which had been no small task. Even though Gene wanted to go back to sleep, he was too excited. He wanted to talk with Darwin—he had so many questions. He wanted to ask him about his voyage, how he came up with his theory, some of the many discoveries since, and what life was like back in the 1800s.

Finally, Sylvia said her goodbyes and left the house.

She warned, "Don't forget to lock the door behind me!"

Gene shut the door and locked the bolt loudly enough for his mother to hear it. After watching Sylvia pull the car out of the driveway, Sophie started to giggle.

"Gene, do you realize we didn't have to do any of that to get out of school today? It's Memorial Day!"

"I completely forgot and Mom musta forgot, too!"

They laughed and went to check on their houseguest, who was still in the hall closet, sleeping in a standing position.

"Mr. Darwin, are you okay? I can find a better place for you to sleep," said Gene.

"Oh . . . um . . . no. Actually, I feel quite rested after that short nap."

"How are you able to sleep like that?" asked Sophie.

"I've had a bit of practice the past two days," answered Darwin with a smile. "Actually, I'd love to learn more about your world and read those books we brought back with us. Maybe they'll give me a clue as to how I got here or how I can get back to my world."

"You'll have to wait until you can talk to my dad for that," said Gene. "I'd also love to talk to you about your life and all the stuff you've done."

Gene saw Sophie rub her eyes.

"Still awake? Hey, that was awesome the way you faked your stomach ache . . . Perfect timing."

"I have way too many questions to sleep. However, first, can we get something to eat?" she asked.

"Actually, I can use some tea and, perhaps, something to eat. My stomach has calmed down quite a bit since leaving that place you call the 'crime scene,' but it's complaining of hunger! You don't happen to have any of those delightful morsels called Krispy Kreme, do you? That detective fellow left some behind when he was in earlier; they were utterly delicious," replied Darwin.

"Doughnuts? Yeah, we have some, but not the cream-filled ones; all we have are glazed. I can get you that and some coffee if you'd like," offered Sophie.

"Yes, please, and thank you so much. I want some more time to peruse the books you left on the table—they look quite interesting. I'm also very curious as to how my theory has withstood time. I hope it has been proven."

⚗ ⚗ ⚗

Darwin sat down at the kitchen table and picked up a book to read.

"Do you know what happened to my coat?" he asked.

"I took it to wash it," answered Gene. "So what do you think of the books?"

"All these books refute every portion of my theory. I don't quite understand all there is to know about cell biology, but I can grasp the concept that the cell is far more complicated than ever we thought in my day. I wish I had known some of this information. I don't think I would've been so quick to abandon the faith of my dear wife. Perhaps, even my father—who first put the idea of evolution into my mind—would've come to different conclusions as well."

"Wow, you read fast if you've read all that so far!" exclaimed Gene with admiration. "So how did you come up with your theory of evolution?"

"Oh, that's a long story. The idea of evolution had been around for quite some time, but no one had put forth how it might have happened. In my day, belief in God as Creator solved everything—no need to think about how things came to be. Poof! God did it."

"Well, right or wrong, your theory has to be studied by every kid in the U.S.—in the world, probably. You've caused us a lot of home-work assignments!"

"Chores at home?" asked Darwin.

"Yeah. Reading assignments to do at home and those stupid papers to write for the next time we have that class."

"Ah, yes. Thinking is good for the mind."

"Not always so good for the emotions," mumbled Gene.

He remembered the turmoil thinking about what he did or did not believe had caused him.

"So tell me about your voyage on the HMS *Beagle*. That sounds like it was quite the adventure. Our textbooks tell us a lot of what you saw on that trip that led you to come up with your theory."

"Ahh . . . yes, that life-altering voyage. Quite frankly, what I remem-ber most was the seasickness! Oh, dear boy, how many days I spent with my head over the railing. That is, when I could leave my bunk! My poor bunk mate; how he must have detested the smell!

"But if you don't mind, can I avail myself of your facilities?" he asked. "You may have to show me again how your modern apparatuses work. Fascinating . . . just fascinating!"

"Sure. No prob," said Gene.

He showed Darwin the facilities. Sophie went into the kitchen to see what she was able to find for breakfast. When Darwin joined them at the table, Gene and Sophie had already eaten a bowl of cereal. They offered some to him as he looked at the box.

"Thank you, but the doughnuts and coffee will be fine."

"So, Mr. Darwin, I'm doing a report on your theory of evolution. I have so many questions. Like, how did you come up with the idea? What did you discover on your voyage? What was it like to be on a ship and travel the world? And—"

"Hold on," interrupted Darwin. "I'll tell you my story. Let me get some food in my stomach first."

He took a few bites of the doughnut and smiled.

"As a boy, I was fascinated by different bugs and animals—I actually collected beetles. I wanted to become a country clergyman so I could observe and collect my specimens. When the chance for this trip came, I begged my father to let me go and to help finance it. I knew it'd change my life. I dreamed of doing something big, and, I confess, not having done so well in university, I really wanted to do something to impress my father.

"I was officially the captain's companion, but I saw it as a chance to explore and collect more specimens. I wanted to have the biggest and best collection of specimens. In this, I wasn't disappointed. I saw creatures I had only read about and some no Englishman had ever laid eyes on."

Gene asked, "What was the weirdest or strangest creature you saw?"

"Let's see." Darwin took a deep breath, sipped some coffee, and looked into the distance.

"I do believe it was the giant skeleton we found on the coast of South America, in Patagonia. It turned out to be similar to a sloth, but four or five times as large."

"Wow!" Sophie and Gene said in unison.

"I also saw it as a chance to think through many things I had learned in university about theology that, well, just did not sit well with me, especially the issue of good and evil. The captain and I had many great discussions about that, as well as certain crew members and I. At first, I was appalled by their lack of manners and belief in anything. Yet as I learned their stories and realized what a good life I had compared to many of them, this issue of good and evil and why bad things happen to good people didn't leave my mind.

"I'm sure all the days at sea when I was so sick, when I could only lie in my bunk and smell those obnoxious odors, didn't help me have a very positive outlook. So I decided to just concentrate on my science. After all, that's what most intrigued me and where I hoped to make my mark.

"What I saw and discovered filled me with fascination. I'd sit and talk with deckhands for hours when they were not busy. The stories they told me were delightful and helped me to find unique and perplexing creatures. Sometimes I felt they were just pulling my leg, but then I'd find fossils of creatures that defied the imagination. They were like nothing that existed anywhere else.

"My mind ran wild with images of what they might have looked like. I confess my imagination also took control a little too much when we made camp in the jungles where no starlight came through the trees. Sounds I had never heard filled my head with visions of all kinds of monsters. At those times, I even believed I sensed evil lurking among us, but when the day came, there was always a plausible explanation.

"I was also fascinated by the geography. I had just received a new book by Charles Lyell about theories of geology and how the present explains the past: the earth is really quite old. Formations resulted from slow processes, which take thousands or even millions of years to form the structures we see today. I thought he made a lot of sense. More sense than many of the biblical stories."

"Yeah, we know all about Lyell and his theories," interrupted Gene.

Darwin paused a moment to take a sip of tea and finish a glazed doughnut. Gene watched him.

"So do you like coffee or tea better?" asked Sophie.

"No, get back to your story," insisted Gene.

This is far better than reading about Mr. Darwin's voyage.

"Actually, my grandfather felt time explained even how living things changed. I began to wonder how Lyell's theories might apply to living things. After all, even the Greeks believed the earth had always existed.

"When I got too bogged down in philosophy, I concentrated on that which I could see and feel. I noticed so many different species, and even found new ones. Spending a lot of time around the sea, I especially became fascinated with the sea creatures, even the ones most others ignored like the barnacle. There was a lot to learn.

"But the first thing I had to do was to get specimens, prepare them as I had been taught, and get them back to England lest my friends and colleagues not believe all the wonderful discoveries I was making. It was at Punta Alta where I saw my most fascinating fossil: a creature that had to be at least ten feet tall but similar to a sloth, which I already mentioned.

"I had a chance to explore the Santa Cruz River. The geologic formations I saw fit perfectly with the theories Lyell presented about long spans of time forming such enormous valleys. No force in nature could've been powerful enough to cause that. Unfortunately, we couldn't make it to the mouth of the river, although we tried all we could think to do.

"Then it was time to drop Jemmy off with his people. Jemmy was a savage from the tip of South America whom the captain had brought back on the last trip and educated in England. The captain hoped Jemmy and his two companions would return to their homeland to educate others. Unfortunately, we learned that didn't happen; Jemmy went back to being a savage . . . such a shame."

"Yeah, but can you imagine how hard it must've been for him? He wasn't that old," said Sophie.

"Indeed it was. I guess he just hadn't evolved far enough for the training to take hold," said Darwin.

"Or maybe he just couldn't take the teasing from the other kids in his homeland. You have to admit, you British had some uncool fashions," added Gene.

Darwin protested, "Exactly what's wrong with our fashion? I think it's this time that has some strange fashions. It'll take me a long time to understand them!"

"Fashion, smashion . . . Just get back to your trip," said Sophie.

"After Patagonia, we had to go around the tip. I thought I had gotten over my seasickness, but it came back with a fury. Being seasick, freezing, and fearing for your life—I wanted off that ship so badly. Never did I ever want to go sailing again! Yet we survived, although just barely.

"Then it was on to more discoveries. I became so excited over these, I temporarily forgot the seasickness."

"Wow!" said Sophie. "I've never got to do anything exciting like that!"

"Exciting, yes, but there's such a thing as too much excitement," replied Darwin.

"You can say that again," Gene piped in.

"I did get to go to Niagara Falls once, but Mom thought I was too young to ride the boat into the Falls!" added Sophie.

She picked up a family photograph of her in front of the Falls to show Darwin.

He asked, "Niagara Falls? Why does that sound so familiar? Ahh, that's where Lyell went. He believed Niagara Falls was a prime example of his theory of long periods of time. According to him, the Niagara River was eroding at about one foot a year. If one calculated the length of time to erode the seven miles from Lake Ontario, well, you must come up with tens of thousands or even hundreds of thousands of years for it to have eroded that much!"

"Nuh-uh," interjected Sophie. "The tour guide said they measured the erosion rate of at least five to six feet a year. That's before the engineers did whatever it was they did to keep it from eroding."

"Really?" asked Darwin.

He started to ask another question when he noticed something strange.

CHAPTER 31
DNA AND DESIGN

Darwin glanced at the pictures on the shelves and walls that reflected the Kysen family's travels. He noticed the picture in one frame kept changing on its own.

"What's that?" he asked in astonishment.

"Oh, that's just a digital photo frame of some of our favorite photos," replied Gene.

"How does it change like that?"

"It's designed to do that. I dunno exactly how it does it. I just know you take pictures with your digital camera, then take the SD card from the camera and put it in the slot in the frame, turn it on, and *voila!* Pictures!"

Gene demonstrated by taking the SD memory card out and replacing it. Darwin simply shook his head.

"Astonishing, utterly unbelievable. Something that small can do all that?"

"Yeah," said Gene. "Like I said, we've come a long way since your time."

Darwin was speechless. He looked at the other pictures and picked up one of Gene wearing a green shirt and holding a pickaxe in one hand and a rather large fossilized tooth in the other.

"Where's this from?" he asked.

"Oh, that's from Gene's Boy Scout trip out West. He's so lucky. I wish our Girl Scout troop had done something that fun!" Sophie said with a pout. "Instead, we sold all those cookies to go camping someplace cool and wound up going an hour from here.

"We didn't even do much hiking or outdoor stuff. Just crafts and listening to a bunch of women telling us how far we women have come. Bleh! I wanted to do the real camping stuff like Gene did with his Scout troop!"

"Yeah, it stinks to be a girl!" Gene teased. "If you were a guy, you coulda camped out in a tent in five-degrees-below-zero weather and cooked your water just to get a drink, or you coulda trekked fifteen miles—loaded with camping gear—in ninety-degree heat. Loads of fun."

Sophie hissed, "Oh, shut up."

She was obviously jealous of her brother's adventures.

"All you do is complain, but I know you had lots of fun!"

"Maybe just a little," Gene admitted with a sly smile, "but to answer your question more precisely, Mr. Darwin, that photo was taken in Utah at Dinosaur National Monument. They've found a ton of dinosaur fossils bunched up in the rocks. They let us dig for fossils and I found that giant tooth. They said it might've been from a Tyrannosaurus rex!"

"Dinosaurs were just beginning to be uncovered in my day. Have they discovered a progressive trail of forms?" Darwin asked with growing enthusiasm. "I remember someone had just uncovered the fossils of what appeared to be a transitional form of a giant reptile bird. Archaeopteryx, I think, is what they called it."

"Nah," Gene replied. "Actually, they haven't, but the paleontologists were excited about such a big find of bones 'cause now they can catalog and describe more thoroughly all the different dinosaur fossils. They even found dinosaur babies still in their eggs! The guide told us they think they might even be able to extract some DNA from some of the bones!"

"DNA?" Darwin asked. "What's that?"

"DNA? Deoxyribonucleic acid, or something like that. It's the stuff that tells scientists what we're made of and who we're related to," said Gene.

"Fascinating; I'd love to visit a place like that! Is that place very far from here?"

"Kinda. It's like a two-day drive. If you fly, it takes about six hours."

"A two-day journey isn't that far. We took a two-month journey up the Santa Cruz, but, like you, I wish we could fly like the birds. I even tried to invent a flying machine once. Have flying machines been invented?" he asked with hope.

"I keep forgetting you're not up on all the technology we have. Not only have flying machines been invented, but planes have also been invented that fly so fast they've actually broken the sound barrier! That's what I want to fly in next."

"So you've actually flown in one of these flying machines?" Darwin asked incredulously.

"Sure," replied Gene, "just a minute."

Gene ran to his room to get a photograph album and a model plane off his desk.

"I used to put model planes together. Now I like to build muscle cars."

"Cars with muscles?"

"No. That's just what they call them because they're the kind of cars real guys—macho dudes—like to drive!"

"Macho? Dudes?"

"Guys who are tough and want everyone to know it," replied Gene. "I'm really gonna have to be careful about what I say, aren't I? Anyway, this baby . . . uh . . . jet is a beauty. It's an F-14 Tomcat military fighter capable of going up to speeds of Mach 2—quite an improvement over earlier models, especially the Wright brothers' prototype airplane," Gene explained.

He showed Darwin pictures of aircraft throughout the century.

Sophie sat down, put her head on one hand, and said, "You'll have to excuse my brother. He gets overly excited when it comes to his hobbies."

Gene ignored her comment and continued.

"As I was saying, each design gets more complex as new discoveries in mechanics and physics are made . . . and they're designed for different purposes. See, this one has an engine with more torque for carrying heavy loads like tanks and heavy artillery. This engine is for speed. Mach 3—three times the speed of sound!"

"But that's impossible!" exclaimed Darwin.

"In your day it was impossible, but each new aircraft design gets progressively more complex and faster or more powerful, whatever it's made for."

"Kinda like my theory of evolution whereby each species gets more complex," Darwin stated with excitement. "This proves my theory of common descent!"

"No, not quite," interjected Sophie. "Each plane is *designed*. Engineers create new designs and make the new aircraft from it. My dad showed me how each aircraft maker has similar designs so you can tell which company made it.

"Like us and all God's creation. We're designed for different purposes: dogs, mice, fish, apes, and humans. We have similar designs because we're made by the same Engineer or Designer—common design, not common descent!"

"Creationists believe in stasis of species," Darwin replied, "and I proved species do change and adapt to their environment."

Suddenly, he bent over and groaned.

"Are you okay?" asked Sophie with a trace of panic in her voice.

"Yes, yes. I just have stomach pains now and then," he said, in obvious pain. "Continue with the discussion."

Then a moment later, he straightened.

With a smile he said, "As I said, stasis of species is illogical, given the evidence."

"What's 'stasis of species'?" asked Sophie.

"That's the belief that once God created a species, it never changes or adapts to its environment. Yet we know that's not true because you can breed traits you want into dogs or plants!"

As she ran to her room, Sophie replied, "Wait."

Gene said, "Actually, I'm not sure what I believe about this because my science teacher has spent a lot of time showing us the different structures and how they are similar. There's a lot of similarity between species in their structures. My science book is full of them."

"All right, I got it here," said Sophie. She was breathless from her sprint to her room and back.

"In this magazine—this is something I never knew—it says creationists do accept that there are changes within species, and this article is about frogs in Africa or something where they discovered such changes. They call this microevolution and know it happens, but it's only within the species and never results in a completely new species. It's macroevolution—your theory, Mr. Darwin—creationists reject. But, yeah, you're right that in your time that's what creationists taught. Since Mendel's experiments and all we've learned about genetics and DNA, we now know how and why it happens."

"Oh, wow!" said Gene. "What magazine is this?"

"It's called *Creation,* and it's put out by a group called Answers in Genesis. When you first talked about your project with evolution and all, I asked my youth leader about some books and stuff 'cause, after all, I study the same books as you. Although I believe God created us and all, it does get confusing when our textbooks tell us something different than our parents and church teach us."

Gene stood looking at the article as Darwin read over his shoulder. "This is cool. Can I have this for my research?"

"Sure," replied Sophie. "I got it for you, but I got so interested in the articles, I wanted to read it myself first."

"So who is this Mendel, and what's DNA again?" Darwin asked.

"Oh, Mendel was a monk who did research on flower varieties and showed that plants have genes, or genetic material, which guide each plant as it develops and give it different characteristics," Gene explained. "So if you cross a red rose with a white one, you can get a red rose or a white one. Then if you take two white flowers that came from this cross and pollinate them, you might wind up with a red rose, but that'd be because the flower had dominate red-flower chromosomes."

Sophie interjected, "DNA is part of that genetic make-up. As a matter of fact, everyone's DNA is so unique they can use it to help solve crimes and identify perps. They do it every week on *CSI* on TV. That's a really cool show."

"Perps?"

"Oh, perpetrators . . . and before you ask, *TV* stands for *television*. It's a box that has all kinds of complicated stuff inside to let us watch movies, which are moving pictures with sound," added Sophie.

"I see," Darwin replied with skepticism. "Back to DNA and chromosomes; where does one find them?"

"They're a part of every cell in our bodies. The cell is really quite complex."

"But the cell is so small. How can it contain all that?" he asked.

"Because it's all super, super small. Just like the memory card for the camera can hold hundreds of photos, the cell is jam-packed with everything it needs to survive and replicate itself. I think in your day microscopes weren't strong enough to magnify the cell to the degree necessary to see all those little parts. We now have electron microscopes," replied Gene. "Here, take a look at my textbook."

Gene picked up his backpack and unzipped it. Instead of textbooks, all the papers he and Sophie had picked up before leaving their father's office were inside. The sight of them made Gene stop. He pictured his father in those prison outfits—it reminded him of why they went to the lab.

Sophie saw him staring at the book bag and asked, "What's wrong, Gene?"

He turned to show her what was in the bag.

"Oh no! Did we lose some of Dad's papers?"

"I don't think so," he said. "It's just . . . well . . . just that . . . ahh, forget it."

"Are you sure?"

"Yeah, but, hey, you know what? All this talk about DNA—if you were at the scene of the crime, Mr. Darwin, your DNA and your fingerprints are there. You can help us free our dad!"

Sophie's mouth opened as she realized the possibility of freeing her father.

"Quick, we gotta call Mom!"

CHAPTER 32
NEW LAWYER

Sylvia felt extremely foolish when she arrived at work and realized it was a holiday.

Oh well, since I'm here, might as well get some work done and see if any lawyers will answer their phone today.

🝳 🝳 🝳

Sylvia breathed a sigh of relief as she listened to the new lawyer. It had taken dozens of telephone calls and hours of research to find a capable lawyer she felt might listen to her. Several lawyers recommended a plea bargain without asking questions. This was all new territory for her, having been burned once by assuming that lawyers were equally qualified. She had a newfound belief in asking questions, lots of questions.

"I think I've heard it all now. They have your husband sitting in jail on a murder charge, and the victim isn't even dead?" asked John Phillips. "All they have is circumstantial evidence?"

Sylvia explained, "Yes. Basically, this detective—Mr. Cousins or whatever his name is—has a gut feeling. He's so sure Ted is guilty he got the judge to deny bail at the pretrial."

"Do you mean at the pleading . . . when a defendant pleads not guilty or guilty?" interrupted Mr. Phillips.

"I'm not sure. I'm new to all this. Does it matter?" asked Sylvia.

"I'll look into that. Go on."

"All our previous lawyer did was object with a quote from some rule. When the judge scheduled another pretrial conference, our lawyer was over half an hour late. He didn't even have a prepared brief like the judge asked!

"He rambled and stuttered so much, the judge quit listening and denied bail on the basis that the charges had merit. I was so upset. I don't know if I was angrier with him, the detective, or myself! I should've realized he wasn't any good and ignored the friend who recommended him. He didn't look successful, and I did pick up on a slight stutter, but I figured if he passed law school and the bar, he must be able to do okay when he's in court or, at least, he must be able to write well.

"I was so emotionally distraught, I just felt pressured into getting anybody. I've never needed a lawyer before; the pretrial was in less than twenty-four hours!"

"Don't feel too bad. Unfortunately, you aren't the first person to come to me irate about Cory Brylan's ineptness. Sometimes he does worse for a client than having no lawyer at all. I don't know how he ever got his license to practice. However, what's done is done. Let's focus on what we can do.

"Okay, now what's the situation with your son? I'll need to talk to him too. The key is to fight on the basis of the forced entry and violation of your Fourth Amendment rights. So here's what I want to do and what I'll need from you," Mr. Phillips stated.

As Sylvia listened to this lawyer's plan, she began to feel some hope. He sounded much more like he knew what to do. She still had plenty of room on her Visa, and if it cost them their house, so be it! She left the office $3,000 poorer but more focused since she now had a plan of action.

Sylvia felt hope for the first time in days. Her emotionally exhausted body began to revive, despite the long drive to get to their new lawyer's office. It was worth it to get her husband out of jail.

CHAPTER 33
UMBRELLA BEATING

Sylvia pulled into the driveway, put the car in park, and sat a moment after turning off the ignition. She had not realized how upsetting finding a lawyer might be, but her muscles were making their presence known.

I'll take a nice soak in the tub before the kids get home from school.

"The kids!"

She had forgotten they were both at home sick. Hopefully, it was just cafeteria food. She did not need any more bills at this time.

Forget the bath, I better check on the kids.

She got out of the car with her shoulders slumped and she began her mental checklist of what needed done. She put the key in the door and pushed it open. She saw Gene's shadow out of the corner of her eye as she took off her jacket.

"Gene, I think I got a good lawyer this time. You need to talk to him right away."

The deep, gruff voice that came from the shadow was not Gene's. She froze. A scream formed in her throat but was unable to escape. She forced her body to straighten up. She looked at the shadow. This was not anyone she knew or, from his appearance, wanted to know. She was scarcely able to breathe.

"You must be Mrs. Kysen," Darwin said. "Glad to make your acquaintance."

Seeing her big black umbrella in the corner, she grabbed it and screamed, "Who are you? What have you done with my kids?"

She swung the umbrella left and right, not caring where she hit him or if she hit him. Then she started poking him with the tip of the umbrella, forcing him to back into the living room.

As she did this, she yelled, "Gene! Sophie! Are you here? Are you okay?"

The man screeched, "They're fine! Ouch, ouch! Stop, please!"

Gene and Sophie appeared and yelled simultaneously, "Mom, Mom! Stop! Stop! That's Charles Darwin! Stop!"

"Gene! Sophie! You're safe!" Sylvia screamed.

The umbrella popped open. She threw it to the side and grabbed her children in a giant bear hug. She saw her kids looked unharmed, signed with relief, and gave them another hug. She looked at them and back at the stranger, who still had his arms in a defensive pose as he kept his distance.

"Charles who?" she asked, completely baffled. "And why should that make a difference? Why is this stranger in my home? Kids, I thought you knew better than to let anyone into the house when your dad and I are not here!"

"But he's not a stranger. We know very well who he is, and so do you . . . and best of all, he can help us get Dad out of jail!" said Gene with excitement.

"But I just hired a lawyer for your dad; he's already filing paperwork to get your dad out of jail."

Then Sylvia turned to the stranger and added, "I'm sorry for your trouble, Mr. Charles . . . whoever, but I already have a lawyer and won't be needing your services. Uh-hum . . . Sorry about the umbrella beating, but you're in my house without adult permission."

"Mom, listen. You're not getting it!" Sophie cried. "He's not a lawyer. He's a witness, an incredibly famous one too. He can help get Dad out of jail because he saw what happened!"

"A witness? That's great, but how . . . where?"

Sylvia slowed down to let Gene and Sophie fill her in on their discoveries as they moved into the living room to sit down.

"Guys, I don't know what to say. It's great someone was there to witness what happened, but the part about how he got there and who he is . . . Well, I just don't see anyone believing it. As a matter of fact, I see it hurting us because no one is going to believe any of this. I'm not sure I believe it," Sylvia stated.

She eyed Darwin with a combination of awe, disbelief, and distrust.

"But, Mom, they gotta investigate. Surely they can test his story and see that it's true!" Gene protested.

"Yeah, like on *CSI*. They can test for DNA," Sophie added with confidence.

"Sophie, dear, that's TV. I don't know that it's as easy in real life," Sylvia replied.

"Can't you at least call the lawyer and see what he thinks?" Gene begged.

Sylvia thought for a moment and then picked up the telephone.

"At this point, anything is worth a try."

CHAPTER 34
WITNESS

"When you said witness, I assumed you meant a credible witness!" an incredulous Mr. Phillips said. "The prosecutor will rip him to shreds! I don't even believe him."

"But can't it help in some way? I mean, he was present and witnessed, even caused, the situation. Can't we do DNA tests or something to at least prove he was there without going into who he is or how he got there?"

Sylvia found herself using the same argument her daughter had used on her. It was meeting the same rejection she had originally given it.

"Mrs. Kysen, let me explain some things to you. In a legal proceeding we have what are called evidentiary standards of proof, which means the level to which a thing needs to be proven true," Mr. Phillips explained with obvious agitation. "They are (1) some credible evidence, (2) preponderance of the evidence, (3) clear and convincing evidence, and (4) evidence beyond a reasonable doubt. This witness doesn't even meet the 'some credible evidence' standard!"

Determined to find a way to get the truth presented, Sylvia countered, "Well, let's just start with his claim he was there. First, there should be a way to establish another person was at the scene. Second, he claims Mr. Agnossi fell and he tried to offer assistance. Isn't there anything in the evidence to suggest this alternative, rather than the detective's impulsive assumptions?"

Mr. Phillips replied, "Actually, we can try to establish there was another person present. I haven't looked over what the prosecution has as far as hard evidence. I'll see if your guy's story checks out with any unrevealed facts. We can present him as a homeless, mentally challenged individual who thinks he's Charles Darwin. That might explain why, other than looking for a warm place to crash, he might be attracted to a university.

"I know from past experience sometimes when a detective, and this one in particular, thinks he has an open-and-shut case, the hard facts are few and far between. The more I think about this, the more I like it. I'll get back to you when I have more. In the meantime, let's schedule an appointment. I'm going to transfer you to my secretary."

With that done, Sylvia hung up the telephone and looked at her kids with a smile.

"Okay, I need your story one more time. This time, I'll have some specific questions for you, Mr. Darwin or whoever you are."

"You still don't believe me, do you, ma'am? Well, I suppose I might not believe myself either if I were you. As a matter of fact, I still don't believe myself, and I know I am who I say. I fear I'm really losing my mind!" Darwin said and shook his head.

"You know, Mom," interrupted Gene, "I think I know how we can prove Mr. Darwin was there and witnessed everything, even if no one believes he's who he says!"

As Gene explained his idea, everyone nodded in approval.

CHAPTER 35
A CREDIBLE WITNESS

TUESDAY, MAY 26

At 5:30 A.M., Gene's alarm buzzed—the excitement from missing a day of school disappeared when he looked at the time. As he reached to shut off his alarm, he actually found himself wishing he had to go back to school rather than to his appointment at Mr. Phillips's office.

Thirty more minutes of sleep, and then I'll get ready in ten minutes.

He hit the snooze button and then remembered his plan. He forced himself to get up.

Gene arrived at Mr. Phillips's office at 8:59 A.M. along with his mother, Sophie, and Darwin. The building was huge. He pushed the button to take the elevator to the fifteenth floor and noticed they were not even close to the top. He was as awestruck as Darwin, who appeared slightly pale as the elevator rose.

"One minute to spare," said Gene to Sylvia. "I told you we'd make it on time."

"No thanks to you!" said Sophie, who had come along as a potential witness. "You complain about me taking forever in the bathroom!"

"A guy's gotta look nice. Never know who you might run into."

Gene immediately thought about Alexis. He knew the probability of running into her in a distant city, on a school day, was absolutely nil. Yet a small part of him still hoped for the impossible. He imagined the elevator door opening to reveal Alexis, sad and looking lonely—she would raise her head, see him, and smile. In his daydream he envisioned himself saying the perfect greeting to get her to laugh.

He was distracted from his daydreaming by Darwin, who was grasping the rails inside the elevator. His eyes were wide and he appeared to be holding his breath. Darwin had stopped to look at everything from the parking meters to the elevator buttons. Gene looked at him and shook his head.

Darwin noticed and asked, "What?"

Gene looked at Sophie and they laughed.

"In here," said Sylvia.

As they exited the elevator, she pointed to a door with fancy lettering on it. Walking quickly and purposefully, she entered the office and held the door open for her more reluctant companions. She gave her name to the receptionist, and then they took their seats on plush leather chairs.

"Hey, Mom, wouldn't these be nice in our house?"

Gene smiled as he got comfortable. Before his mother was able to respond, another door opened, and Mr. Phillips invited them inside his office. At that point, Darwin was not the only one looking around in bewilderment. The inner office looked extravagant: nice, comfortable chairs; a matching sofa; and a huge desk with ornately carved legs adorned the office with plenty of space left over. Two green plants filled floor planters next to a window with an incredible view.

I can see for miles!

After introductions, Mr. Phillips jumped right to the issues. He told them he had filed continuances on Gene's case to focus on Ted's case scheduled for court soon. When they secured his freedom, it would be easy to get Gene's case dismissed. Mr. Phillips was confident the pretrial motion would be successful; however, as a lawyer who had seen many twists in cases, he always had a contingency plan in place.

"Mrs. Kysen, I do need to tell you the prosecutor has offered a plea bargain. If you plead guilty to one of the charges, the other will be dropped; he won't ask for any detention time. Gene has the two charges: obstructing official business and resisting arrest. If you don't accept the plea, they'll consider adding a third charge: injuring an officer. He wants an answer before your husband's case. What do you think about that? Are you interested?"

"That's blackmail!" Sylvia shouted. "Not a chance. Gene did nothing wrong. I don't want Gene to lie and say he did something he did not do, but Gene has a say as well."

Gene looked at his mother, who was still tense with emotion and smiled.

"I'll listen to my mom on this. I want all this over with and I know my dad is innocent . . . and I know we have a witness!"

"Very well. I thought you'd say that, but I did have to present it to you. Now let's talk about our witness. Gene, tell me more about your witness. Why do you believe him?"

"Sure. Mr. Phillips, this here is Charles Darwin, the author of *The Origin of Species.* I didn't believe him at first, but after he told me what he saw, and being at the lab myself, I believed it made a lot more sense than what that detective guy says happened."

Until then, Darwin had been so quiet it was easy to forget he was there. Gene saw Mr. Phillips give Darwin a look to size him up.

He's probably wondering if this really is Charles Darwin, or a homeless, mentally challenged individual.

"I take it a lawyer in America is the same as our solicitor?" Darwin inquired. "I'm pleased to make your acquaintance, sir . . . and, please, call me Charles."

"Yes. That's correct . . . and it's a pleasure to meet you, Charles. Please be seated. Now have you ever had any experience in a court of law?"

"No, sir, I haven't."

"The first thing you must be prepared for—if I put you on the witness stand—is getting a fierce cross-examination from the prosecutor. So let me hear what you saw: Why were you in the room? How did you get in?"

"Well, sir, as to how I got into that room, I simply cannot tell you. One moment I was looking for my coat because I felt a chill at the approach of a storm outside. It seemed to come from nowhere, ruining an unusually beautiful day. The next moment I was in that room. There was a bright light; I thought it was a lightning strike.

"There was also a noise—very strange, such as I have never heard before. It hurt my ears. The light changed from a bright white to blue to a red glow. When my eyes finally adjusted, I saw a man. At the time, I was not even sure it was an earthly being! I thought my heart had finally given up on me and I had died.

"I still do not understand. I thought I was dreaming. Sometimes I still think I'm dreaming. Everything is so strange to me!"

Darwin stopped talking and reflected on that night.

"I had been excited because I had just received some woodcuts from a German scientist—pictures to prove my theory."

His statement caught Gene's attention. He knew who the scientist had to be. He looked at Sophie, who looked back at him with her eyes and mouth wide open. She was obviously thinking the same thing. Gene started to ask Darwin about the identity of the German scientist.

This has to be more proof this is the real Mr. Darwin.

Mr. Phillips's skeptical voice interrupted Gene's thought. "This prosecutor is going to tear your witness to shreds."

Then he turned back to Darwin and said, "Just tell me exactly what you saw and what happened. We'll try to avoid how you got there."

Thirty minutes later, the group sat in silence as Mr. Phillips stared out the window.

"Okay. Step one: we need to get Mr. Darwin, I mean, Charles some new clothes to present a credible witness. Nothing fancy, even second hand, but we need to update his style," Mr. Phillips said. "Actually, I think we have a wardrobe for just such clothing emergencies; we'll see if we have his size. Maybe we can save you some money.

"Then I'm going to go through this pile of evidence. I have a feeling some important things are missing. I have a private investigator; he does very thorough work. I'm going to have him do some things for me."

Then he looked sternly at Gene.

"I think we should avoid using any of your testimony on being at the lab after it was taped off. That can get you into more trouble, Gene, but I have some ideas brewing about how to handle this."

Mr. Phillips turned to his intercom and asked his secretary for the new intern, Noah Jeffries. A moment later he appeared. Gene had to stifle a laugh or any expression of his feelings when he saw Noah. The young man was professional enough, but he wore a bow tie and his pants were high-waters. With a name like Noah, Gene wanted to ask him if he was expecting a flood.

"Noah, will you take Charles to the closet to see if we have any jackets that fit him?"

"Yes, sir. Come this way, Charles."

"Um, excuse me, Mr. Phillips, is there a bathroom I can use?" asked Sophie.

"Sure. Just go ask my secretary."

"I think I'll go with you," Sylvia said. "That is, if you have no further questions, Mr. Phillips."

"I'm finished for now, but I want a chance to speak with your son some more about Charles Darwin. Is that all right with you?"

Sylvia looked at Gene, bit her lip, and said, "I think that'll probably be a good idea."

Since Gene was the only one in the grand office with an important lawyer, he felt intimidated. Mr. Phillips sensed Gene's discomfort.

He smiled and said, "Your mom said a lot about you when we talked on the phone. I'm glad to finally meet you. I can say this case with you and your dad is the most interesting and bizarre case I've taken on in all my twenty-some years of practice . . . and I've had some strange cases!

"Now that I have had a chance to speak with Charles, I feel he's either very crazy or the real McCoy. Either way, he's very knowledgeable of Darwin's life and theories. I'll have to talk to your dad and ask him more about this machine."

Gene simply smiled and nodded his head. He had not thought about the situation like that before, but his dad had created a time machine. He had to tell his friends about that, which reminded him of a question he had for his lawyer. However, Mr. Phillips continued talking and Gene felt compelled to just listen.

"I confess the idea of time travel has fascinated me since I was a boy. I just can't help but think how marvelous it'd be to have a time machine to go back in time to see what really happened in a lot of criminal cases, mine particularly. I'll bet we'd find out we got it wrong a lot of the time. I sincerely believe there are a lot of innocent people in prison, serving time for crimes they had nothing to do with. I also think we'd discover we let a lot of guilty people go free."

"Yeah, this whole thing is bizarre, but you know, my dad says there's a scientist who wrote his doctoral thesis on the possibility of time travel. He suggested the basics of a machine to travel forward in time. The problem, at least according to this guy: it's only possible to go forward in time. Not to the past. I know I want to go back in time a few months at least. That is, as long as I can know what I know now," Gene said with a nervous laugh.

"That's a big Amen. It won't be any fun to go back in time if you had to keep repeating the same mistakes. Oh, if we could repeat the past with the knowledge we've gained from the future! That's why I'm so thankful to be a Christian. At least, if we can't go back in time and do things right, at least I know I have a Savior who doesn't hold my mistakes and sins against me forever. It's nice to be able to get forgiveness and know we can learn from our pain and suffering and Christ can make it all work out for good."

Gene must have shown surprise in his expression because Mr. Phillips added, "Oh, excuse me. Your mom is so open about her faith; I just assumed you share it. So do you believe this, Gene?"

"What? That Jesus helps us?" Gene was blown away to hear a highly-educated stranger talk so openly about his faith.

For all the fancy things in his office, this guy seems all right.

Mr. Phillips was so open with his personal beliefs—the kind Gene usually kept to himself—that Gene felt at ease answering him.

"Yes, and not only that He helps us, but that He can also make everything better than it was before," confirmed Mr. Phillips.

"I want to; I've been taught this. You know . . . things get complicated. Some things just don't seem like they can ever work out," Gene said. "Like with my dad. He's lost all this time at work which he's not getting paid for. He'll probably even lose his job no matter whether he's proven innocent or not.

"At least, that's what my mom is worried about. It makes me wonder if Mr. Darwin doesn't have it right. I mean, what kind of loving God makes you go through all this pain? Mr. Darwin lost his mom when he was a kid and then had a couple of his kids die while they were still young."

Mr. Phillips asked, "So you think God caused all those bad things to happen? What's your evidence?"

"I dunno if God caused them, but can't He stop bad things from happening . . . and what do you mean, what's my evidence?" Gene asked. "You can't prove or disprove things you can't see."

"Well, that depends on how you define *prove*. We often conclude things and events as fact because the logic or reasoning behind the thing is so compelling," Mr. Phillips explained. "In other words, based on all we know, a thing just had to happen that way."

Gene had to stop and think the concept through. The discussion had a lot more meaning to him at that moment than it might have a couple of days before.

How do I know whether or not God caused this, was able to stop Dad from getting arrested, or make something good come from all this? What good can come from having to repeat eighth grade because I can't get all my reports done? How do I even know if there's a God or not?

He felt bad for even doubting God existed. God was so ingrained in his thinking because of how he had been raised, but what sounded good in theory did not seem good when in the middle of so much pain.

Gene and Darwin had had the same conversation. He was angry at what he had seen his father go through. When Gene thought about it, he became angrier and hurt for his parents more than himself. It really had not sunk in how much trouble he was also in.

It's actually kinda cool to have a little adventure and have people realize I'm not just a Mr. Goody Two-Shoes!

When Gene considered what Darwin had gone through, it was no wonder he did not believe there was a God who cared what happened to mere mortals. Gene had not realized all the bad things that had happened to Darwin—he might have read about some of those things, but it did not have the same effect as when he actually got to know him as a person and felt his pain. When Darwin had explained his reasoning behind his theories, it made a lot of sense.

Gene had confused himself. One minute he questioned Darwin and his theories; the next he questioned God and all he had been taught.

Why can't I just make up my mind?

Gene shifted his weight, gazed out the window, and thought about how insignificant he felt at that moment.

Is there really a God?

He felt Mr. Phillips staring at him, waiting for him to continue.

"So, Mr. Phillips, can you prove God exists? Or rather, what is your proof of God . . . and what do you think of Mr. Darwin's theory of evolution? Doesn't it make a lot sense? Doesn't he have logic and solid reasoning on his side . . . facts, which are hard to disprove?"

Not knowing what he believed at this moment, Gene was unable to stop himself from blurting out all his doubts. Mr. Phillips just smiled.

"Slow down. These are great questions, Gene. God isn't afraid of our questions. He gave us our inquisitive minds, and you must ask questions—the right questions—to get the right answers. Let's simplify and organize this issue and the assumptions behind them.

"At the heart of the creation-evolution debate is the question of whether or not God exists. Then, if there is a God, what's God like? Is He good and loving with a purpose for each of us as Christianity teaches, or distant and uninvolved as other religions teach? How can a loving God allow us to experience pain? Can pain ever be good?

"Is the evidence of pain and suffering in this world against God, or is there a god-like entity that created life and let evolution take over? Did we evolve by pure chance—from totally natural mechanisms that leave us existing with no purpose, plan, or reason?"

"Wow!" Gene replied. "How can you get all that from one statement?"

"I'm a lawyer. That's what we do. We make everything longer and more complicated, but with good purpose. You have to get at the heart of the whole evolution-creation-intelligent design debate by understanding all the issues and defining terms. However, before I continue, what do you believe? Your mom informed me you've been working on a term paper about this very issue."

Put on the spot at that moment, Gene was not sure. That was the problem: he was not sure about anything. Once he had been sure about God as Creator and a loving God who cared about humans enough to send His Son, Jesus, to save all mankind. That is, those who accept and believe in Him. When he was in his science class, he had begun to believe and accept what his teacher taught. After all, it was school and his teacher had gone to college to learn far more than most people about the subject, even his Sunday school teachers and youth pastor.

Then he got hold of books that showed the errors of evolution and the fact there were no facts to support evolution. That made him angry to think he had to learn such garbage in school. Then he talked to Darwin. Listening to the guy who had actually started the whole controversy, Gene found himself going back and forth.

What do I believe? What's truth and what's garbage?

Before Gene could respond, the telephone rang. Mr. Phillips held up a finger to motion for Gene to wait, and then he picked up the telephone. Mr. Phillips listened and nodded.

Finally, he said, "No. They want you to prove your point at trial."

Mr. Phillips smiled and looked at Gene.

"That was the prosecutor in your case. He's not happy you refused his generous offer."

"Generous?" scoffed Gene. "They're the ones at fault. They shoulda never busted into my house like that."

"I agree," said Mr. Phillips, "and we'll have to go through their case against you in much the same manner as I'm questioning you about your presuppositions and defining terms. So back to our discussion about creation; do you believe there's a God?"

"I dunno what I believe at this moment," Gene heard himself admit. "Mr. Veritas, my youth pastor, told me evolution is just a way for people to justify a life of sin, especially sex-type sins. Because if there's no God, then there's no moral law, and then we can live as we want. He says we have a God-shaped vacuum that tells us that's not true.

"Then there's Eric, a kid a year above me who used to be in my church, who says that's just a way for the church to control us. They make us afraid we'll suffer punishment in some afterlife. He says he used to always feel guilty, so he quit going to church, did what felt good, and just went by what his gut told him was right and wrong. His life got simple and fun. His motto is 'If it feels good, do it.'

"Also, my science teacher says evolution isn't a theory anymore, but a fact. He says all scientists accept this fact. After all, he says, look at all science has done for us since scientists accepted Mr. Darwin's theory. He says carbon dating can prove the earth is millions of years old. Even the way they measure stars shows the earth is that old 'cause it takes thousands of light-years for the starlight to travel to Earth. I don't have a clue how to answer that—do you?"

"Actually, I do," answered Mr. Phillips. "We'll come back to that. What can you defend the Genesis account of creation with from what you know so far?"

Gene replied, "At the hospital I got all these books against evolution and learned there really aren't as many facts for evolution as a lot of people say. There's the Cambrian explosion when a bunch of creatures appear suddenly; there are no 'missing links' in the fossil records; there have been a lot of hoaxes when people made up fossils; Stanley Miller's experiment was a failure; the archaeopteryx is just a bird, not a missing link; and the flood can explain a lot about geologic things.

"Some of the creation books, however, admit the earth is millions of years old. Some say it's only seven to ten thousand years old. So how does that go with the carbon dating and starlight? Oh, yeah, I forgot about Haeckel's embryos. Did you know they were fakes? Textbook publishers have known that for like . . . a hundred years!"

"No, I didn't. Tell me more," Mr. Phillips answered. He leaned forward on his desk to let Gene know he was, indeed, very interested.

"Well, somebody else—I forget who—did a comparison of the same animals with newer technology, and they didn't see any similarities. Hey, I think that man who'd given Mr. Darwin some woodcuts because they didn't have photographs like we do today was Haeckel!"

"Interesting," Mr. Phillips said. "That'd be a point in his favor. Not many people know that."

Gene said, "See, it's stuff like that—he knows all this stuff about Mr. Darwin's life!"

"I'm not totally convinced yet. It can still be an act."

"I don't think so," Gene replied. "When I talked with Mr. Darwin, we argued about a lot of things, but when I listen to him talk, he's pretty persuasive. He said he did lots of research and saw evidence of changes. I'm not good at remembering facts, so I can't remember half of what I've read. Then Mr. Darwin started talking about all the bad stuff that happens in the world and what has happened to him.

"I go back to thinking about what's happened to me and my family lately. It doesn't matter what my brain thinks. I just feel angry and want to chuck it all and leave it to someone else who cares. Then I feel guilty for wanting to give up on God. Sheesh, I can't believe I'm telling you all this stuff. You musta put truth serum in my pop or something!"

"I wish I were able to do that," Mr. Phillips said with a laugh.

"So you're the lawyer. What are your proofs? Tell me how I deal with all this stuff. Is there enough evidence for God or does evolution win . . . Why does it even matter what I think?"

Gene was silent for a moment. He could not believe he was opening up to a stranger. He also had not even realized he felt so much turmoil until it started pouring out of his mouth.

"I can tell you've done a fair amount of reading and a great deal of thinking. That's good. Now you can come to a wise decision, but let me start with why it's important what you think and believe. You see, beliefs lead to actions and actions have consequences. Your friend, Eric, believed it didn't matter and quit going to church, quit living right. That happens to a lot of young people.

"Yet you haven't heard their stories after a few years of living however they want . . . I have. A lot of my clients didn't think it mattered how they lived: which drugs they took or what they did to get those drugs. That is, until the law caught up with them. Then they learn: it isn't what they feel is right or wrong; it's what the law says is right and wrong. Granted, the law is harsh and impersonal.

"That's why the offender needs a lawyer who can inform the court of circumstances to lessen the offense. I think many Christians focus so much on the law, and what is or isn't right, they miss the advocacy—that is, the lawyer—part. Jesus is our advocate or lawyer. He puts mercy into the law and goes before God to ask for mercy.

"You can also think through beliefs and actions to their logical conclusions. Did you know Hitler was a big fan of evolution? So were Stalin and Lenin. Millions are now dead: over six million Jews in World War II, over twenty million Russian dissidents under Stalin, and I don't recall the number killed to squash the freedom movement in Tiananmen Square in China . . . and so on. Did it matter what these men thought?"

"Geesh, I never thought of it like that," Gene replied. "Are you saying evolution causes people to do really horrible stuff? I never made that kind of connection."

"Most people don't; they go by their feelings and accept ideas without thinking them through. They simply accept what they're told and go on to the next fun thing. And to answer your question, I'm not saying all people who accept evolution do horrible stuff like Hitler, but think about it. Any belief system that doesn't value life sets the stage for people to do horrible things to each other. Even if they don't kill others themselves, they often soothe their consciences with reasons to justify not doing anything either."

Gene fidgeted in his seat and said, "But Mr. Darwin is a nice guy. He sure didn't want people to get hurt from others misusing his theory."

"Nice people can have seriously flawed ideas that lead to bad consequences. As I said, that's why it's so important what a person believes, especially about God and whether or not He created us."

Mr. Phillips paused a moment. He sat back in his chair and rubbed his chin with his thumb and index finger.

"I can see you get tripped up by the idea of pain and suffering and how a loving God can let that happen, but that's not the way it's supposed to be. God made a perfect world for us. He wanted us to enjoy it, but He wanted us to choose to love Him. After all, real love can't survive if you have to please the other person to be accepted. Real love loves even when that love isn't deserved or even returned. God is also a righteous God.

"Justice demands sin be punished. That's easy to accept in a court of law if you're the victim or the one who's been wronged. Yet when you're the wrongdoer, you want mercy, not justice. So realize sin—ours, someone else's, or systemic sin—committed by imperfect men causes pain. God made us and understands all of life. He commands us to do things for our benefit that allow us to live a good life, but He gives us choices.

"Sometimes my wrong choice causes unintended consequences for those I care about. However, that doesn't mean God caused the pain. That's part of living in a fallen world. Honestly, though, when you think about it, wouldn't you rather believe all that pain is going to bring about something good . . . that you aren't suffering for nothing . . . that there's hope of a better life?"

Gene thought a moment and answered, "I guess when you put it like that . . . yes; I'd rather have something to hope in and for."

Mr. Phillips continued, "So logically, it makes sense to believe in God, but we have more than just logic or warm, fuzzy thinking. We have evidence that an intelligent entity—even if you don't want to accept the God of the Bible—has designed us. Recent scientific discoveries in molecular biology absolutely demonstrate the complexity with which we've been designed. Even the smallest one-celled creature is a complex system of nanotechnology—a system whose parts must all be present or it can't exist.

"Michael Behe has written a book entitled *Darwin's Black Box* that explains this. He uses the example of a mousetrap to show how it must have each part—no part of the trap has a purpose until it has been assembled as a whole. From there, he takes you to the world of molecular biology to show how complex living things really are."

Gene said, "Wow, sounds awesome. You'll have to explain it to Mr. Darwin. We actually have that book. When Mr. Darwin saw the title, he was very curious about what was in his black box. I think I want to read that book."

"That's not all. A new book by Stephen Meyer entitled *Signature in the Cell* makes a wonderful case for DNA as a complex computer program. It's also a fantastic book in that he shows the history behind ideas. As a creationist, I admit a lot of evolutionary ideas sounded so ridiculous I did not understand how an intelligent person might accept it. Of course, that's how evolutionists feel about creationists, so we argue and convince no one because we miss the assumptions and philosophies behind ideas.

"For example, have you ever wondered why evolution caught on so quickly despite no fossil evidence or explanation about how the first life form came into being? Even Charles admitted his theory didn't explain how the first life form became a living entity. During his time, scientists didn't know much about the cell or possess powerful enough microscopes to see the cell's complexity. They thought it was just a gelatinous glob consisting of inorganic chemicals mixed in the right way with the right form of energy, and bingo—life!

"The theory of evolution was quite popular with the intellectuals of the day, who were also introduced to new philosophies in behavior and politics. Marxists loved this theory, even though the concept of sudden, noticeable changes fits their political theory of change by revolution a little better. If there was no creator, then it was up to man to change his world. Atheists saw immediately how the theory could be used to their benefit too.

"Also, have you ever noticed how evolution seems to explain everything? If there were transitional fossils, they would be proof, but a lack of these fossils also supports evolution. The changes are too small to notice or simply haven't been found. A theory so broad it explains everything is really no explanation at all. Take Einstein . . . When he came up with his theory of relativity, he made bold, specific predictions others were able to either prove or disprove.

"I can go on for quite some time about this subject. Do you want me to or do you need a break?"

Gene looked at the clock. It had been thirty minutes.

"Whoa!" he said. "Look at the time! My mom's not gonna get billed for this time, is she? She warned me you lawyers charge by the second!"

Mr. Phillips laughed and said, "No. I'm not charging for this! It's been fun for me to have this discussion. This subject is my passion, and I see its applications to my work all the time. To think I'm involved in a case where I might get to show Charles Darwin the error of his thinking is reward enough for me!"

Gene was startled when a deep voice behind him said, "I want to show you the error of your thinking too."

It was Darwin. Behind him Sylvia and Sophie stood with surprised looks on their faces.

How long have they been there? How much of this private conversation have they heard?

CHAPTER 36
THE TRIAL

TUESDAY, JUNE 9
9:00 AM

Two weeks later, Sylvia, Gene, Sophie, and Darwin were at the court-house dressed in their Sunday best. From hopeless despair to an optimistic plan of attack in just under two weeks had been no small feat. Yet the group felt ready for the trial about to take place. It had taken a lot of work to prepare Darwin, who kept bringing conversations with Mr. Phillips back to his theory. He had become somewhat defensive after overhearing how their lawyer felt about evolution.

Gene felt ready for the trial. He felt confident and nervous at the same time. He did not know how that was possible, but it was how he felt.

He had finally finished his science report and mailed it to his teacher. It wasn't his best work. He didn't have time to add all the cool stuff he'd learned.

Hopefully, it'll be accepted, 'cause I don't want to fail. Summer school would be the pits. But if Mr. Phillips fails, I won't have to worry about that. I can't let myself think about that. Think positive.

Gene literally shook himself and looked around the courtroom, observing the people sitting around him. Most men were in suits or dress slacks. Some actually wore raggedy jeans and T-shirts. Gene found himself thinking those people simply had no class. Then he wondered what those people felt about him.

How are others judging me and my family?

He was dressed in black Levi's and a dark blue shirt with a dark blue-and-red-striped tie. He hated ties, but his mother said he had to wear it.

The past week had provided several opportunities for rehashing parts of the discussion about creation which Gene had had with Mr. Phillips. Several of those talks had been with Darwin. Gene did not know if Darwin had changed his mind about anything, but he felt a growing confidence about what he believed. More important, he no longer felt he had to have an answer for every question that arose in order for his faith to stay strong. He was aware of how similar preparing his mind for a trial was to evaluating the evidence for creation or evolution.

The most important thing to do was check presuppositions. Then he could evaluate the facts to see which theory or idea was more consistent with the evidence. Also, he needed to watch for logical conclusions. He should have put more examples of that in his report.

Oh well, too late now.

"All rise!" the bailiff cried.

A short, stocky man entered the courtroom and instructed everyone to be seated. He looked decades past retirement.

⚗ ⚗ ⚗

The Honorable Y. W. Goode was the first African-American judge in this county; he was proud of it. Judge Goode had spent thirty-three years practicing law, and his short-cropped hair was almost completely gray. Yet he still had hair; he was proud of that too.

The trial could be long and drawn out, given some of the complex issues before him. However, depending on the defense lawyer's strategy, it could be short and sweet.

I can always wish for a short, uncomplicated trial.

Judge Goode quickly dispensed with the preliminaries. The jury had been selected and needed the final admonition to presume innocence and remember the prosecutor had to prove his case. With that finished, he informed the prosecutor to begin.

Prosecutor Paul Mangil rose slowly and strolled to the jury box as if he were in deep thought. He gave the jurors a very serious look and began.

"Ladies and gentlemen of the jury, we're here to ascertain the guilt or innocence of one Theodore—Ted—Kysen in the Felony Assault of Damien Agnossi on May 22, 2009. As we present the facts of the case, you'll see a premeditated attempt on the life of Mr. Agnossi made by his lab partner, Mr. Kysen, with intent to kill him. The planned attack resulted in serious bodily harm.

"On that night Mr. Kysen did argue with his boss. Witnesses will verify the argument turned violent. That violent rage turned into an almost deadly assault. Apparently, Mr. Agnossi had interrupted Mr. Kysen in an attempt to sabotage the experiment. Then, Mr. Kysen lured the victim into the laboratory where he almost killed him.

"We have phone records that will establish the two had communicated that night. We have eyewitnesses who put Mr. Kysen at the scene, and we have the testimony of the victim himself who wrote the name of his attacker in his own blood at the scene.

"Mr. Kysen's motive is simple. Since Cain and Abel, men have argued over places of favor and gain. Both men wanted the same job. It carried a lot of professional prestige and financial gain. At risk: not only this potential gain, but also disfavor and loss of professional status . . . perhaps even employment. Murders have been committed for lesser motives than the defendant had.

"Ladies and gentlemen, we believe you'll have clear and convincing evidence of the guilt of Mr. Theodore Kysen. Thank you. Your Honor, the prosecution turns the floor over to the defense."

John Phillips rose to present his opening statement. He also walked over to the jurors, and then he smiled and greeted them warmly.

"Ladies and gentlemen of the jury, you've been asked here to decide if the prosecutor has enough evidence to demonstrate a murder attempt actually took place. I want to remind you, it's the prosecutor who has the burden of proving what he's saying is true. The law requires you to start with the presumption the defendant, Mr. Ted Kysen, is innocent of the charges brought against him. Just because Prosecutor Mangil makes a statement or an accusation doesn't mean it's true.

"Can you think of a time when someone accused you of something you didn't do? Something you may not have even known occurred until you were accused of committing it? If so, how did you feel? Now consider if that accusation put you in the defendant's place. Wouldn't you want your jurors to start with the presumption you were innocent? Wouldn't you want them to evaluate the truth of every accusation?

"Ladies and gentlemen, not only is Mr. Kysen innocent of attempted murder, he wasn't even present when the unfortunate accident took place. Yes, ladies and gentlemen, what happened—although tragic—was an accident. We also have evidence based on facts, not circumstances or wild theories as the prosecutor will present. We also have an eyewitness. As a matter of fact, we have an eyewitness, present at the scene when the accident took place, who will verify Mr. Kysen had already left the building."

Prosecutor Mangil rose as if given an electric shock and shouted, "Objection, Your Honor, we haven't been informed about this witness!"

Mr. Phillips smiled politely at him and then at Judge Goode and replied, "Your Honor, this witness is listed under *other possible witnesses* and has only recently come forward. We had to verify facts and information."

"This notice was sent to the prosecutor's office as required."

Mr. Phillips walked back to the defendant's table, picked up a file, and rifled through it.

"Here's the delivery confirmation, Your Honor."

Mr. Phillips handed the paper to Judge Goode.

"I also want to bring to the attention of the court that the prosecutor's pretrial motions to suppress certain facts have unwittingly caused him to overlook crucial information available to his office all along."

After reading the proffered documents, Judge Goode stated, "Objection overruled. Defense has established its compliance with the rules of evidence. The defense may continue."

Prosecutor Mangil sat like an obedient attack dog in silence; his frustration was obvious.

Mr. Phillips continued, "Ladies and gentlemen, my client and his boss did have their share of professional disagreements, but the hostility stopped there. If being angry at your boss is sufficient ground to be charged with an attempt on his life, I fear our prisons can't be built fast enough to hold all the people who would then be convicted. Think of the new taxes needed to build those prisons. Why, I daresay no one would be left to pay those taxes or, for that matter, guard those prisoners."

Everyone in the courtroom laughed and nodded their heads. There were also several sheepish grins acknowledging the fact they too could just as easily be the one on trial.

"So remember your job today is to evaluate every statement and accusation and then compare it with the proffered evidence. Ask yourself what the unstated assumptions are and make sure the prosecutor earns his pay. Make him convince you beyond a doubt that what he says happened has evidence to back it up. Ask yourself how you'd feel if you had been arrested for a crime you didn't commit. How would you feel?

"Not just arrested, but savagely attacked by an armed garrison of battle-ready troops in the middle of the night! Not even knowing that anything had happened to your coworker, let alone that you were the suspect for a serious crime against that coworker. How thorough and critical would you want your jurors to be?

"Ladies and gentlemen, when we're finished presenting our evidence to refute these groundless accusations, I'm convinced beyond a shadow of a doubt you too will not only agree that my client is innocent, but that he has also been treated shamelessly and unprofessionally . . . and his basic constitutional rights were inexcusably violated."

With that, Mr. Phillips sat down.

Gene was impressed. *This guy had everyone laughing and empathizing with Dad in a matter of minutes.*

He felt they were going to win. He just hoped the jury felt the way he did.

How can they not?

The evidence against Ted was circumstantial, while the evidence for him was solid. Gene looked around and hoped Darwin was sitting in the hall with the other witnesses. He wanted to be out there with him; however, as part of pretrial motions, all references about what Gene was accused of that night were suppressed. So Gene was not supposed to be a witness, even though he had helped get the necessary evidence.

Judge Goode said, "Mr. Mangil, you may call your first witness."

"Your Honor, the prosecution calls Solomen Cozen, Ashland County detective."

The bailiff had the detective raise his right hand. Detective Cozen swore to "tell the truth, the whole truth, and nothing but the truth."

"Hey, Mom," whispered Sophie. "I thought they were supposed to use the Bible and swear on it to tell the truth. Why don't they have a Bible?"

"Probably because too many cops were struck with lightning," Sylvia whispered back.

Gene was shocked.

Mom . . . being sarcastic?

What she had said was more like something he would say. Gene scarcely kept from laughing out loud when he saw Sophie's stunned expression turn to a muffled giggle. He noticed Judge Goode looking at them and put his head down to regain control.

After a few preliminary questions to establish the detective was who he said he was and what his credentials were, Prosecutor Mangil began to ask more specific questions about what led Detective Cozen to arrest and charge Ted with the crime.

"We were notified a man was being treated at the scene for apparent stab wounds and had lapsed into a potentially fatal coma from loss of blood. The victim was being prepared to be taken to the emergency room. Me, Officer Dressler, and Officer Downy went to the laboratory at the university and were the first ones on the scene," reported Detective Cozen.

"What did you discover when you arrived there?" asked Prosecutor Mangil.

"The emergency squad had just stabilized the victim for transport. He was pale and barely breathing into the oxygen mask. They had stopped the bleeding from the cut on the victim's arm, but you could tell it had bled a significant amount.

"In the lab we noted many bottles of unknown substances. Broken glass was on the floor next to a stand that held experimental substances. On the floor we also discovered a scalpel-like object covered with blood. Most ominous, on the floor next to where the victim was lying were also the letters *t-e-d*. Obviously, the victim had spelled out the name of his attacker prior to passing out from loss of blood."

Prosecutor Mangil held up a sharp instrument inside a clear plastic bag so every member of the jury was able to get a good look.

He asked, "Can you identify this instrument as the one you discovered at the scene, covered with blood?"

"Yes, sir," Detective Cozen replied. "It is."

"Tell me, what kinds of tests were done on this weapon?"

"Objection!" yelled Mr. Phillips. "Your Honor, it's only an alleged weapon to an alleged crime. There's another explanation which we'll present later."

"Very well," Judge Goode replied. "Objection sustained."

Prosecutor Mangil looked as if he were going to say something and then thought better. He shook his head as if in disbelief that there could be any other explanation and then continued in a slightly sarcastic tone.

"What kinds of tests were performed on this *alleged* weapon?"

"We did the usual. Blood tests confirmed it to be the victim's blood. Too much blood was on the handle to get any good fingerprints."

Prosecutor Mangil pulled out a picture from a plain manila file. He was in a hurry to change the subject because he knew they were able to get partial prints, but the prints did not match Ted's, Damien's, the lab assistant's, or the girlfriend's, who had made the call for help.

While Sal Cozen was a good detective on the stand, he occasionally talked too much and inadvertently volunteered information that might be used to sink his case.

He asked, "Is this a picture of the name you found scrawled on the floor next to the victim?"

"Yes, it is."

"Tell the jury what this says, Sal . . . er . . . Detective Cozen."

Sylvia leaned over to her son and said, "I like the name Sal better. In French, *sal* means 'dirty'."

Gene did not say anything. He knew his mother was agitated, but he had rarely seen her agitated enough to make so many snide comments.

Detective Cozen took the picture and began pointing out the letters. It was not as distinct as he made it sound. The *t* might also have been an *l* and there was a mark in-between the *e* and *d*. Surrounding the letters was a pinkish fluid that looked as if it had spilled and faded the rest of the letters.

It was the first time Gene had seen the pictures. He looked intently at them but did not think it looked like *t-e-d*. Something about the letters tickled nerve endings in his brain. He kept thinking there was something important he faintly recognized but struggled to tell what it was.

He looked at his father, his mother, and then Sophie. Once again, he found himself looking for Darwin but reminded himself his new friend had to stay outside the courtroom because he was a witness. For some reason, the lawyers had asked for separation of witnesses at the beginning of the trial. He had started to ask Mr. Phillips why and then remembered he had already explained that in a trial witnesses remain outside the courtroom to avoid modifying their testimony to match, or sometimes contradict, someone else's.

Gene had worried about Darwin being outside with the other witnesses alone, and so had Mr. Phillips. They had decided Noah, the high-waters guy, would stay with Darwin. The last thing Mr. Phillips wanted Darwin to do was to start telling everyone he was Charles Darwin, author of *The Origin of Species.*

Gene smiled to himself. It was pretty incredible to think the real Charles Darwin was outside the courtroom. Then suddenly, it dawned on him what looked so familiar about the picture of the name in blood. Gene looked again and figured it out. He needed to get Mr. Phillips's attention. He was not seated close enough to say anything, at least not without another stern stare from Judge Goode.

Gene wished he had some paper with him. He saw Sophie's notebook on the chair next to him, picked it up, and ever so carefully ripped out a sheet of paper. Sophie and Sylvia looked at him and shushed him. He wrote what he thought the name was supposed to say.

Yes! It works.

He had to get the note to Mr. Phillips. If it had weight like a rock or football, he could just toss it.

Hmm . . . a football.

Gene began to fold the paper. Sophie stared at him with a look that begged to know what he was doing. In a few seconds, Gene had made a perfect little triangle—a football.

Here's the most important touchdown of my non-athletic career.

Gene held the triangular paper with one tip on the chair in front of him. With one finger on the top, he aimed and flicked it with his other hand. The miniature football landed on the defense table and then slid off to the floor.

Oh, no!

He saw Mr. Phillips and his father look at each other, around the room, and finally to the floor. Ted looked back at Gene.

Who else could it have been?

He gave his son a look that said, *What? Why?*

Gene pointed to the floor and mouthed, "Get the paper football!"

Ted tapped Mr. Phillips and pointed to the floor. Mr. Phillips noticed the triangular paper. He made sure neither Judge Goode, Prosecutor Mangil, nor the bailiff was looking and then put his foot over the paper football. He pulled it closer to him and then bent over to feign scratching his ankle and picked it up.

When Mr. Phillips did not immediately read the note, Gene began to involuntarily bounce his foot up and down. He always did this when he was nervous or agitated. He had to put his hand on his knee to stop the tremor. Sylvia and Sophie glared at him to stop.

Come on, Mr. Phillips, open the note! he began to mentally beg. *First, you unfold it, and then you read it.*

Finally, he saw him open the note. Gene let out the breath he did not even realize he had been holding. It seemed to take forever for Mr. Phillips to react.

When Prosecutor Mangil turned the witness over for cross-examination, Mr. Phillips rose and asked to approach the bench. The judge waved them forward.

"Your Honor," Mr. Phillips said quietly but with urgency. "We request a fifteen-minute recess. Some new information has come to my attention."

"Since I can use a bathroom break, I'll grant the recess," Judge Goode replied.

He looked as though he was pondering some great and deep issue.

"Any objections, Mr. Mangil?"

"No, sir. I can use a break as well."

♟ ♟ ♟

In a crowded side room, Mr. Phillips, Sophie, and Sylvia stared at Gene.

"I believe you," said Mr. Phillips, "but this goes back to our witness credibility."

"Yeah, but isn't it more a matter of what *he* thought? Does it really matter if Mr. Darwin is who he says if Mr. Agnossi thought he was staring at Charles Darwin?" Gene said. "I mean, Mr. Darwin is . . . was his hero. He has pictures of Mr. Darwin in his office. Even if Mr. Agnossi thought it was an actor dressed up to look like Mr. Darwin, might he not still try to write *Charles Darwin*?"

With all the passion and confidence he could muster, he continued, "Besides, didn't you tell me how important it is what a person believes . . . that beliefs affect actions?"

Mr. Phillips looked at him. Then he smiled.

"You know, you're getting pretty good with your logic. I think you're on to something. I wish we had more than fifteen minutes, but we don't. So we need to get back."

Just as they were ready to walk out the door, they ran into his intern, Noah.

"Mr. Phillips, we struck pay dirt . . . Look here!"

"Noah, please tell me you're holding the missing security disc!"

"I am! Undeniable and exculpatory evidence!"

Gene interjected, "What does *exculpatory* mean? It sounds bad, not good."

"Oh, *exculpatory* means something good. It means it'll prove your dad is completely innocent!"

Mr. Phillips said to Noah, "Tell me more."

Noah handed the evidence over to Mr. Phillips.

"It has fingerprints that appear to be our Mr. Darwin's. It also shows exactly what happened . . . just as Mr. Darwin said it had!"

Gene looked at Noah and smiled. They high-fived each other and followed Mr. Phillips back into the courtroom. Gene wanted to shout in victory, but he controlled himself. Instead, he let his mother hug him.

As soon as the judge entered and called court back into session, Mr. Phillips stood.

He said, "Your Honor, I want to make a motion to submit exculpatory evidence we've just uncovered. May I approach the bench to show you?"

He showed Judge Goode and Prosecutor Mangil the disc and explained what was on it. Immediately, Prosecutor Mangil objected and quoted references to federal rules of evidence and criminal procedures that prohibited the introduction of new material during a trial.

He said, "Your Honor, I need time to review this and verify prints and a host of other details. I motion to suppress this evidence. How do we know it hasn't been fabricated?"

"For one thing, it has doughnut crumbs and cream—evidence your number-one detective used it for a plate!" Mr. Phillips snapped.

"Gentlemen!" interjected Judge Goode. "Unfortunately, Mr. Phillips, I do agree with Mr. Mangil on his citations. For now, I'm going to rule this disc as inadmissible. I don't want to turn my courtroom into a circus with sudden, manufactured evidence."

"But, Your Honor—"

"I've made my decision. Mr. Phillips, unless you wish to be cited for contempt of court, I suggest you return to your seat."

Gene saw Mr. Phillips was furious. When he whispered to Ted what Judge Goode had said, he saw his father suddenly sit up straight and drop his jaw in utter disbelief. Then Mr. Phillips turned, looked at Gene, and shook his head.

It was Mr. Phillips's turn to cross-examine Detective Cozen.

How can Mr. Phillips do a thorough job when a crucial piece of evidence is inadmissible?

Sure, he had prepared for cross even without the disc, but to know it existed, that it was exculpable material, something that would prove without a doubt the innocence of his client, clouded Mr. Phillips's mind with anger.

How can this judge, any judge, not allow hard evidence? This is a clear violation of Ted's rights!

He had to save that thought for later—an appeal, if necessary. As much as he detested this part of law, he had to go with the rules.

"Detective Cozen," Mr. Phillips began, "tell me again, what hard evidence did you have to arrest my client? So far, I have only heard circumstantial presuppositions, at best. First, my client had the misfortune of working with the deceased . . . True. Second, they wanted the same job . . . Allegation, but probably true. Third, they had differences of opinion about how to handle issues that arose . . . Also true.

"This is hardly proof of motive for murder. The allegations of fiscal misconduct were made by my client, but there has been no proof of what or who did it. There's an alleged weapon without my client's fingerprints, and now you try to read my client's name into some illegible scribbles on the floor."

"Those allegations have been verified by witnesses and point to a pretty strong motive for revenge," answered Detective Cozen.

"What about these letters on the floor?" Mr. Phillips walked over and picked up the photographs. "What did you say this letter was?"

"That's a *t.*"

"Looks to me like it can be a an *l* or *I.* Isn't that a possibility?"

"I guess to the untrained eye it can look that way."

"Oh, so you're trained in handwriting analysis?"

"No, sir, I just have experience in these things."

"Do you also have experience in fabricating evidence?"

"Objection!" Prosecutor Mangil shouted.

"Sustained," replied Judge Goode. "Jury, you're instructed to ignore that last statement."

"I withdraw the question," said Mr. Phillips. "One last set of questions. Did the lab have any security system?"

"It had a card lock and digital surveillance."

"Did you review the surveillance video?"

"We tried to; it was recorded to a disc that's missing."

"What steps did you take to find the missing disc?"

"We followed procedures—"

Prosecutor Mangil immediately stood and asked permission to approach Judge Goode's bench.

When both lawyers were before him, Prosecutor Mangil said, "Your Honor, Mr. Phillips is going down a path that'll lead to an area you've already ruled inadmissible."

"Your Honor," Mr. Phillips interjected, "having security is standard for most labs, and the question is valid. It also allows for questions pertaining to thoroughness of the investigation."

"Mr. Mangil, this time I'll have to rule in favor of Mr. Phillips's argument. He has a right to ask these questions, but I warn you, Mr. Phillips, you're not to use this as a pretext to insinuate you have the missing surveillance footage."

Gene wished he was able to hear the discussion between the lawyers and Judge Goode.

How can a judge not allow proof Dad had nothing to do with the crime?

Gene wanted to shout out something when Detective Cozen said they did not find any surveillance disc. Yet he just sat there . . . fuming.

Mr. Phillips asked him a few more questions. Then he told Judge Goode he was finished for the time being but wanted to preserve his right to recall the witness.

"Mr. Mangil, do have any questions for redress?" asked Judge Goode.

"Yes, sir, I do," he replied and rose from his chair. "Mr. Cozens, I want to draw your attention to the comment the defense mentioned about allegations of fiscal misconduct. What did you base this upon?"

"We talked with a colleague who told us Mr. Agnossi was worried about inconsistencies in the fiscal report."

"Is that all?"

"No, sir, we found paperwork at the scene of the crime showing the figures didn't add up to the same report sent to the grant foundation."

Prosecutor Mangil walked to the evidence table and picked up a plastic bag. Inside was a single sheet of paper.

"Was this the paper you found?"

"Yes, sir."

"Where did you find it?"

"Under the accused's desk, in a corner—it's obvious evidence of fiscal misconduct."

"Objection!" yelled Mr. Phillips. "Opinion."

"Objection sustained."

Gene looked at the paper, unable to breathe. He was not certain it was the same piece of paper he had seen drop from his father's desk. However, when Detective Cozen said where he had found it, he realized it had to be the same document. Everyone in the courtroom whispered.

Gene did not know how to process the revelation. He saw the unfairness of the trial: Prosecutor Mangil got to present his evidence, but Mr. Phillips was not allowed to present his.

His evidence doesn't need any interpretation!

The unfairness continued to worsen. The next witness tried to make Ted appear to be a liar and thief. Damien's girlfriend, Marsha Pickens, accused Ted of stealing grant money. First, Gene knew his father would never do that. Second, if he had, he hid it pretty well because he never had extra money.

There has to be another explanation for that piece of paper. After all, it's not the whole report.

CHAPTER 37
THE DEFENSE CALLS . . .

Gene was a little nervous as he waited for Darwin to take the stand. He had not heard everything Mr. Phillips had told his mother about how they were going to handle Darwin's testimony. As far as he knew, they were just going to portray him as a street person who thought he was the real Charles Darwin. Gene did not think it a good idea—something about trying to hide a truth had the potential to turn the whole thing into a big mess.

"Call your first witness," Judge Goode instructed Mr. Phillips.

"The defense calls Sam. . . ."

Not Darwin. Good.

Gene did not listen to all of Sam's testimony or his cross-examination. He was worried about Darwin: not just about what he was going to say on the witness stand, but how he might hold up. Darwin had been acting like he was going to be sick—he had complained of stomach problems.

Finally, Sam, Ted's graduate assistant, completed his testimony. He had done a great job sticking up for him as he testified about how Ted was a great person to work for—kind and honest. When Prosecutor Mangil tried to get Sam to say something to make Ted look bad,

Sam got angry and gave him an earful. Gene thought their exchange was hilarious.

"The defense now calls its next witness," said Mr. Phillips. "Mr. Charles Darwin."

His statement and the ensuing courtroom chatter interrupted Gene's thoughts. He overheard someone behind him laugh.

Then the man said, "This guy must be desperate to call a witness with *that* name. I hear he's a street person."

Gene wanted to turn around and yell at him. Instead, he turned and said, "Shh!"

Darwin walked up to the witness stand slightly bent over. Gene suspected Darwin was indeed still having trouble with his stomach. Then he found himself smiling at the thought of Darwin throwing up all over Prosecutor Mangil.

It'll serve him right!

"Raise your right hand and state your name," said the bailiff.

"Charles Darwin."

Mr. Phillips asked, "Mr. Darwin, where were you on the night of May 22, 2009?"

"I was in the Ashland University lab. I'm not sure how I got there."

"Were you there to get out of the cold?"

"Objection," yelled Prosecutor Mangil. "He's leading the witness."

"Sustained. Rephrase the question, Counselor."

"Why were you there?" asked Mr. Phillips.

"I don't know. I wanted to be someplace safe and warm," answered Darwin. "Did you see this man?" asked Mr. Phillips, holding up a picture of Damien.

"Yes, I did."

"Did you see this man?" asked Mr. Phillips as he pointed to Ted.

"No, I didn't."

"Did you touch anything while you were there?"

"Yes, lots of things."

"Did you ever touch or hold this item?" asked Mr. Phillips. He held up the scalpel, which was still in a plastic bag.

"Yes, I did. I used it to try to help the man in the first picture."

People in the audience began to chatter loudly.

Someone said, "My Lord!"

Judge Goode used his gavel to get everyone's attention. "Order in the court!"

As soon as the courtroom observers calmed down, Mr. Phillips continued. "What happened to the man while you were in the lab?"

"I heard a shrill whirring. There was a blinding white light. I covered my eyes, and when I was able to open them again, I saw a man with poofy black hair. He wore a white lab coat. He screamed when he saw me, and I screamed too. Actually, it would've been comical if I hadn't been so terrified.

"Then the man fainted. I rushed to help him because when he fell, he knocked over several glass apparatuses. I saw he had spilled chemicals of some sort—I don't know what they were. So knowing how toxic such chemicals might be and the need to get them out of one's system right away, I grabbed a scalpel I had seen and made a small incision in his left arm to release the toxic blood.

"The man woke at this, grabbed my hand, and started screaming. I'm not sure of all he said, but I heard him imploring me to get away—I did. I backed away and saw him pass out again. I was afraid . . . He needed help . . . I didn't know where to go. So I opened the first door I found.

"Unfortunately, in my haste I didn't realize it was a closet until I ran into a wall. I must have hit my head pretty hard on one of the shelves."

"Did you lose consciousness?"

"No. Unfortunately, I was quite conscious. My head hurt tremendously, and then I felt quite nauseous."

"Did you hear anyone else enter the lab?"

"Not for some time."

"How long?"

"I can't say. I was rather disorientated."

"Did you see who came in next?"

"No, but I heard them. It was a lady's voice. I heard her yell, 'Damien, baby, Damien! Help . . . Someone, help!' Then I heard some strange beeping noises and the lady's voice saying she needed the police and an ambulance. I don't remember all she said.

"A few moments later, I heard a man ask, 'What's going on? Ms. Marsha, are you all right?' She said she was fine but Damien was hurt and she didn't know what had happened, but she had already called 1-1-9. I mean 9-1-1."

"Did you let anyone know you were present?"

"I started to, but then I felt pain and nausea again and fainted."

"Did you hear the woman call this man by any name?"

"Actually, I did. What was it . . . Warren? Yes, that was it. Warren."

"No further questions."

Gene was pleased that part had gone well. It appeared Mr. Phillips also thought so. Next came the part Gene and everyone else was worried about.

"Please, God," Gene prayed. "Please help Mr. Darwin not say anything stupid!"

Judge Goode asked, "Mr. Mangil, do you wish to cross?"

"Yes, Your Honor, I do."

What happened next was sweet—not for Prosecutor Mangil, but Gene loved it!

Yes, there is a God!

When Prosecutor Mangil started to yell at Darwin and pummel him with questions, Gene saw Darwin was getting sick. Unfortunately, Prosecutor Mangil had not.

"Mom," whispered Gene, "it looks like Mr. Darwin is getting another one of his nervous stomach attacks. Can't our lawyer make the prosecutor back off or get the judge to give everyone a break?"

"Yeah," Sophie piped in. "I think Mr. Darwin is going to get sick!"

"He does look somewhat pale. I think the judge is noticing it now," replied Sylvia.

"Oh, man! They better hurry up and stop things. I think he's gonna hurl!" whispered Gene.

"So you want this jury to believe you were in that laboratory, hiding, while police were investigating the scene?" bellowed Prosecutor Mangil.

He leaned close to Darwin and put his hands on the wooden gate that separated the witness from him.

"Mr. Darwin, if that's your real name, tell us why—"

At that precise moment, Darwin threw up all over Prosecutor Mangil. Gene wished he had an instant-replay button. The look on Prosecutor Mangil's face was one of surprise and utter disgust. The look on Judge Goode's face was one of complete astonishment and then revulsion as he backed away and put his hands up to protect himself from contamination. Mr. Phillips was standing with his hand slightly raised, finger extended, as if frozen, astonished.

The jurors leaned back in their seats, covering their noses and mouths. They looked as if they too might get sick.

Finally, Mr. Phillips asked, "Recess, Your Honor?"

"Granted. Court dismissed until 9:00 A.M. tomorrow," replied Judge Goode.

He quickly exited the court, holding his nose.

Gene and Sophie looked at each other in shock! Then they started to laugh. They tried to laugh quietly at first but were not able to keep from laughing out loud.

There were cross words voiced by a lot of people, but court ended promptly. Everyone rushed to get out the doors. The bailiffs called for a janitor. Prosecutor Mangil simply looked dumfounded, unable to wipe himself off. Darwin was in obvious pain; he seemed oblivious to the commotion he had caused.

"Quick, get to the bathroom and get paper towels!" Sylvia told Gene and Sophie.

CHAPTER 38
TABLE TALK

Later that evening, they all sat around the table, discussing the events of the day. Sylvia sat at the head of the table with her head in her hands. Sophie looked sympathetically at Darwin, who still looked pale. Gene folded his napkin into a little football, just to have something to do. No one had an appetite for dinner.

"It's strange," said Darwin. "All these years I've been seeking a cause and cure for my stomach pain. To discover a headache is to blame is truly amazing."

Then after a pause he added, "One doctor tried to tell me my pain was all in my head. I guess he was right!"

He let out a slight laugh and tried to smile.

"Well, actually it's not quite a headache," said Sylvia. "The doctor explained you have a migraine, which has been reclassified as a central nervous disorder. Most people experience very painful and debilitating headaches, but some people experience only the nausea and vomiting. The trick is to find the catalyst, or what causes the migraine. Sometimes it's a food you ate; sometimes it's just stress. Are you feeling better now?"

"Yes, thank you. That experience with the prosecutor was very stressful. It amazes me a pill that small takes care of such awful distress. Despite how awful I felt at the hospital, I can't help but be impressed by the marvelous advances in medicine. My father and grandfather would've been thoroughly impressed. Father always wanted me to follow in his footsteps—maybe I should've."

"You still can," said Sophie, ever the optimist. "After all, does anyone know if Mr. Darwin can go back to his time period?"

"Wow," said Gene. "I hadn't even thought about that yet. You probably can't go back to your time period. Once, Dad and I discussed the topic of time travel. He'd read a book by a guy who researched that stuff, and the guy felt time travel into the future was possible, but not going back in time. That's impossible."

"Well, quite honestly, I thought any form of time travel was impossible, and here I am!" said Darwin. "While I'll miss my friends and family, I'm so utterly thrilled with all the marvels of this time, I'm quite content to stay and learn all I can!

"Actually, my dear Sophie, I do think you have a good idea. Even if I'm willing to try the machine again, which I'm not at present since there's no guarantee it'll work. I have a wonderful opportunity to see how my theory was proven or disproven. From some of my discussions with each of you and the lawyer, I need to compare my theory with the new discoveries in science. One thing that particularly interests me is this DNA. What does it stand for again?"

"Deoxyribonucleic acid. It's the stuff responsible for the traits we inherit," replied Sophie.

Gene added, "It's also needed to help build proteins, which build muscles!"

He tried to display his new muscles by raising his shirtsleeve to show off his biceps.

"That reminds me, Mom, can you order me some more of that last protein shake I ordered? I think it's finally starting to work!"

"Oh, let me get my magnifying glass," Sophie teased. "I'm not sure I see anything."

"Sophie!" Sylvia admonished. "Don't be so mean. Gene, I do see a difference, and I'm not just saying that because I'm your mom."

"What's in this protein shake?" asked Darwin.

"All the amino acids needed to build muscles, and various vitamins and minerals . . . and carbohydrates so I can put on some weight that'll turn to muscle."

With that, Gene got up from the table and went into the kitchen to get his last can.

"Here. Read this label. It lists all the ingredients," said Gene.

Darwin tried to read the list of amino acids.

He said, "I don't recognize half of these ingredients. How has it been determined what the cells need? How do they even work? In my day, even under our best microscopes, the cell appeared to be a simple piece of gelatinous material with a dark spot in the middle."

"We have electron microscopes, which use electrons instead of light," answered Gene. "They can magnify images hundreds of times more than a regular light microscope. Dad has them in his lab. They're really cool!"

Another thought took root and he added, "Oh. I know. I'll get my science textbook. It has pictures of the cell. We had to study it last grading period."

Gene was so excited to be the one in the know that he knocked over his chair and tripped as he tried to stand. Sophie started to laugh hysterically.

"You might have more muscles, but you're still a klutz!"

"Shut up!" Gene cried out, embarrassed.

"Gene! Are you okay?" Sylvia shouted.

"I'm fine."

He leapt up and went for his book.

"I think I got something that'll help too," said Sophie.

Then she carefully backed her chair out and went to her room.

Darwin shook his head and smiled.

"Those are fine children you have, Mrs. Kysen. They get so excited about science and learning. It reminds me of the days when my children helped me with my experiments."

"Thank you, Mr. Darwin. How many children did you have?" she asked.

"I had seven beautiful children. Sadly, two of them died in childhood. I don't think I ever got over that. Have you had that misfortune, Mrs. Kysen?"

"No, thankfully I only wanted two children, but I have a friend at work who lost a child to cancer . . . leukemia. It was sad. She almost quit work because it was too hard for her to deal with. She's a Christian, and her faith helped her through all the pain, but not without a struggle."

"My dear wife turned to her faith also. She said it helped, but for me . . . well, it just made me angry. Why does a loving God let an innocent child suffer and die?"

"That's a hard question to answer, but it's not God who makes children suffer and die. He does love us, but sin causes all kinds of suffering and death . . . whether it's our sin, someone else's, or systemic. It's a result of the fall."

"Bah! I can't accept that . . . not the suffering of innocent children. Isn't God supposed to be all-powerful?"

"He is, but we can let these things make us better by turning to God for help, or we can let them make us bitter by focusing on our pain."

All Darwin was able to say was "Hmph."

"I don't know what kind of pain you went through; I can only imagine. However, just imagining it causes extreme sadness. My mom died when I was young. It's been long enough now that I can talk about it without it hurting too much, but it took a long time for that pain to fade," Sylvia said. "For a while I was very angry at God.

"Eventually, I realized I only hurt myself by refusing to let God help me. When I did finally ask God for help, He gave me a wonderful sense of relief. Finally, I was able to smile again. It was not just a one-time thing where I said, 'Okay, God,' and I lived happily ever after. Every time I got hurt or angry, I felt the pain all over.

"Sometimes I still got angry and sulked for a few days, but eventually, I learned I was able to choose not to be angry. It still bothers me some days if I let it. Yet I can tell God exactly how I feel and know He still loves me. When I do that, I'm free to live."

"You sound so much like my wife—I'm missing her too!"

Darwin looked up to see Gene standing next to him with his textbook open. He had a look of sympathy on his face. When he had realized the seriousness of their discussion, he did not want to interrupt.

"Let's change the subject," Darwin suggested with a forced smile. "I want to see what your textbooks have about the cell."

"This is a diagram of a cell. You can see how complex it really is. There's the nucleus, the mitochondria, and here's where the DNA is."

Gene pointed at a picture detailing the makeup of a cell. Darwin took the book and looked at the picture with interest. He read the highlighted material.

"Fascinating, just fascinating!"

Just then, Sophie returned with a magazine.

"Here's an article about the cell and how complex it is. Mom, how do you say these words?" asked Sophie as she handed over the magazine.

"Irreducible Complexity," replied Sylvia as she returned the magazine to her daughter.

"What does that mean?" asked Sophie.

"It means a system is so complex it can't be made any simpler and still function as it's supposed to."

"I thought so, but I just wanted to be sure."

Sophie placed her magazine next to Gene's textbook. The room fell silent as Darwin read one article after another. It was so quiet when the doorbell rang, everyone jumped.

CHAPTER 39
THE MOUSETRAP

"Mr. Phillips," said Sylvia as she opened the door, "what a surprise. Come on in out of the rain. I didn't think lawyers made house calls."

"Not usually," he answered. "Thanks for inviting me in. I apologize for coming unannounced, but I'm staying with a pastor friend nearby. I have two reasons for stopping."

"Do you want any coffee? Something to eat?"

"Coffee sounds great . . . I like mine black. No thank you on the food; I just ate."

"Hi, Mr. Phillips!" Gene said. "You're just in time to help us answer some of Mr. Darwin's questions about DNA and why it's so important."

"Maybe you can also help us with this article in my science magazine on ir . . . .re . . . duc . . . ible . . . com . . . complexity," Sophie stammered.

"Just my kind of discussion," John Phillips answered with a smile. "That's one of the reasons for me stopping by. I have some more books for you."

Darwin said, "I've been reading about the cell in Gene's textbooks and how complex it really is—far more than we ever thought in my day! I just started reading about the irreducible complexity of the flagellum. I haven't had time to process how this affects my theory, but I can see the importance of pondering the issue."

"Yes, Michael Behe's mousetrap!" Mr. Phillips said.

"I beg your pardon?"

"Mr. Behe wrote a book about irreducible complexity and used a mousetrap to demonstrate his point. Mrs. Kysen, do you happen to have one?" asked Mr. Phillips.

"There are some in the kitchen drawer. I'll go get them!" Gene interjected.

He jumped up from the table and ran into the kitchen. He was back in moments.

"Here," said Gene.

"Excellent," said Mr. Phillips. "As you can see, there are several parts to this simple contraption. There's the base, spring, trip bar, and hammer. If any one of these parts is missing, it won't catch any mice. Granted, you can use the parts for other things, but no part by itself will catch a mouse."

"Ahh. I think I see the connection. So this author is saying living parts such as cells are also irreducibly complex. In other words, he's saying my theory falls short because for a cell to work, it must have all the parts. In order for the next part to fall into place, it takes a designer. Yes, my wife likes that argument, but I'm not sure. With enough time I think the parts might all come together."

"Natural selection, a process of pure chance, isn't going to know another piece of the puzzle is needed, let alone what piece it is."

"Therefore, you're saying we'll need an all-powerful, all-knowing God?"

"I believe so," answered Mr. Phillips. "However, there are many scientists today who don't want to admit there's a God but are convinced by the evidence there must be an intelligent designer. I believe when the evidence is presented fairly, like in a legal trial, it leads to God. I personally believe the verdict is the God of the Bible, who exists and is the Creator of this world and us."

"That's just your belief," said Darwin.

"It's a belief based on evidence. DNA is the source of information in the cell that's needed to make proteins and reproduce itself. Information can only come from intelligence. Like any computer program, someone has to design it," said Mr. Phillips.

Gene listened carefully to how Mr. Phillips answered Darwin. He never seemed at a loss for words or a good answer . . . and he always was calm. Sometimes Gene became irritated when trying to answer a question because it did not sound right. He thought comparing DNA and computers made a lot of sense.

Darwin asked, "Any what?"

"Oh yeah, I forgot," answered Mr. Phillips, "computers are new to you."

"Hey!" interjected Gene. "Maybe later I can show Mr. Darwin how a computer works. I have a basic program we can play around with."

"Actually, that's a great way to help understand DNA, but first, let's come back to how DNA will help us tomorrow at trial. That's the other reason for me stopping by. Gene, I got to thinking about the information you gave me. That's the first time someone has hit me with a paper football to give me information during a trial—novel idea! I just don't think the judge will agree, so don't do that again, okay?"

"Okay," Gene agreed with a laugh.

"Gene, I think you're right. I do think Damien was trying to write *Charles Darwin*, not your dad's name. When you start with that presupposition, you can see how credible that interpretation is. It adds a crucial element of doubt to the prosecution's theory. When one adds the fact Charles Darwin is Damien's hero, it makes sense. After all, Charles, when I first saw you in my office, you looked just like the pictures I've seen of you."

"Thank you, but I'm not sure that's a compliment. I look pretty disheveled in some of those pictures. Probably, I was having trouble with my stomach at the time. However, it's nice to know someone considered me a hero."

"This is the news I've been dying to tell you. Noah did have the results back from the DNA samples we requested . . . and it's a match. So no matter whether or not people want to believe you're Charles Darwin, this DNA proves you were indeed present! Plus, the fact you told me about the doughnut conversation between the detectives establishes you were present at the time of the crime, or at least very soon after."

"Yes!" shouted Gene, Sophie, and Sylvia in unison.

"In addition, Gene, since you found that other piece of evidence . . . well, I don't see how we can lose. At least, in a fair fight. Needless to say, the prosecutor wasn't very happy about being vomited on—he may try and pull something."

Sylvia asked, "Like what?"

"That is what I've been trying to discover. If he wants to be sneaky, there are some things he can do. So we do need to discuss more strategy. However, if for some reason we lose this, we can still appeal. I do think we already have enough evidence for procedural errors we'll win an appeal."

"But shouldn't the prosecutor realize that?" asked Sylvia.

"He should, but like I said, he was made to appear a fool today. There's no telling what he may try to pull. Even if he knows he'll lose the appeal, he may try to make us go that route simply out of spite."

"But that won't be right!" shouted Sophie.

"Yeah," said Gene, "this is America! Don't we have the best system of justice? I've been praying for you to win, for Dad to get out of jail. If God doesn't answer my prayers . . . I . . . I don't think I can ever pray again! I don't think I can ever believe in Him again!"

"Gene!" Sylvia interjected, "don't say things like that! God will answer our prayers. All of us have been praying for the truth to come out and for your father to be exonerated, set free. Be patient. God doesn't always answer us the way we want."

"Well, I don't want to wait. It's already been too long!" moaned Gene.

He felt guilty about what he had just said.

How can I say I'm ready to give up on God when for the past week my faith has increased?

Gene knew his remark was fueled by his emotions, feelings he had bottled up. Still, it bothered him that he felt that way.

Everyone got quiet. They were all worried. Finally, Mr. Phillips commented.

"Gene, I know just where you're coming from. In my personal and professional lives, I have prayed for God to intervene, to snap His fingers and make things happen for me. After all, I thought, this is a good thing I want done. Yet God's ways are true and right, no matter what we think or want. What I've learned in my personal and professional lives is God will answer in His timing, His way. We need to have a humble attitude and submitted spirit.

"I used to think this approach was being weak, but I've since learned—and relearned—it takes a great deal of strength to hold back. Think of a big, strong warhorse. It has energy and is ready to go, but it won't charge until the command is given. Nor will it run away in fear or turn in any way, except when the rider directs it."

"You mean like the horses in the movie *Braveheart*!" said Gene.

"Yes. That's a great example. A horse easily guided is said to have a soft neck; that's a good thing. At the slightest pressure or command, the horse will turn, even though it's strong enough to throw its rider and do what it wants!

"That's what God wants us to be—strong, but soft-necked. This way, when He speaks in His soft, still voice, we'll be able to detect His leading. Many times I realized God did answer my prayers, but I was too pig-headed to know it. So I had to learn the hard way and suffer the consequences."

"So," asked Sophie, "what you're saying is since God speaks to us in His small, still voice, like He showed Elisha—"

"Elijah," Gene corrected her.

"Yeah, whatever," continued Sophie. "Like I was saying, since God speaks to us in a small, still voice, and not a big wind like a tornado, we need to be submitted or surrendered to His will so we can hear His voice?"

"Precisely," answered Mr. Phillips, "and that takes strength! When every muscle in you wants to tell someone off but you don't because that small, still voice warns you not to . . . that takes strength. Don't let anyone tell you being surrendered to God is the same as being weak!"

"How do you know it's God talking to you and not just your thoughts?" asked Gene.

"Good question, Gene," Mr. Phillips answered. "I think learning to know the voice of God is the most important task of the believer, because sometimes it is just our thoughts. Trial and error—you do something or don't do something you believe God told you and then judge the results. It's taken me a while to learn this, but there are ways to increase the odds of getting it right. One, ask whether or not the voice is consistent with the teaching of the Bible. Two, ask if your heart is right with God—are you truly seeking the truth?"

"Yeah, I've heard that in church. Can you give me some examples of a case as messed up as ours, where it seemed everything went wrong, despite your client being obviously innocent?" asked Gene.

It amazed Gene how this lawyer always turned every conversation into a Bible lesson. He felt like he was in church, but it was one where he was able to blurt out his questions no matter how disrespectful they sounded.

He added, "How about a time when it wasn't so clear? For example, I know the Bible says not to take vengeance and forgive those who hurt you, but this prosecutor wants to put Dad in jail for something he obviously didn't do; I can't forgive him. He's hurting Dad and all of us. I don't think I should forgive him 'cause, after all, he's supposed to represent truth, justice, and all that."

Mr. Phillips looked at Gene with an understanding smile.

"Yeah, that's tough . . . really tough, but it leads to the second reason I came by."

He took another sip of coffee. Then the sound of harps playing came from his pocket. He took his cell phone out to read a message. He looked at Sylvia.

"Just Noah confirming some references I asked him to look up. Mrs. Kysen, you look tired. Should I leave or can we continue this discussion?"

"Sure, why not? I have so much nervous energy I'm not going to bed early tonight," she replied.

Mr. Phillips refocused his attention back to his previous train of thought.

"I can tell you what one client did, despite the unfortunate outcome," he continued.

He shook his head and smiled. However, it was not a happy smile.

"I can tell you about a grandma who got arrested by a SWAT team for simply standing on the stairs in her house."

CHAPTER 40
FORGIVE THEM?

Mr. Phillips took a deep breath and exhaled slowly. He pushed his chair back and propped his right foot across his left knee.

"This client told me her son was having a regular visitation with his son at her house when a SWAT team entered the house to get the boy. They arrested her and her son in the process. Despite showing the police and prosecutor his copy of the joint custody agreement, they still filed charges against her son and her. It was a misdemeanor, but it did carry potential jail time. It was an obvious case of overaggressive policing."

"That's awful! So we aren't the only ones to experience a SWAT arrest?" asked Sylvia.

"No. You'd be surprised how often SWAT teams are enlisted for ordinary, or what should be ordinary, arrests."

"What happened to the grandson?" Sophie asked. "How old was he?"

"I think the little boy was only three. He wasn't harmed physically, but I did discover he had to go through a considerable amount of trauma counseling."

"What did she do?" asked Gene. "Or . . . what did they say she did?"

"It's what she allegedly didn't do. Like anybody would do when awakened to such a commotion, she came down her stairs to find out what was going on. Confronted by several armed officers dressed in black, she froze. The police say she refused to move and their obstruction charge derived from that."

Gene cried out, "I know how that feels!"

Every time he thought about that night when he was confronted by the SWAT team, he felt the fear and confusion, especially the confusion. So many thoughts went through his head that night—it took longer to explain them than to feel them. If this was the example of a time things did not work out for Mr. Phillips, Gene was not sure he wanted to hear it. He wanted a happy ending; he wanted justice.

"Eventually, I saw her later and we got to talking about the case. She told me how she was able to see things in hindsight that she wasn't able to see at the time. She also shared how she had forgiven the people who had harmed her, even the ones who purposefully lied."

"How could she just forgive them?" asked Gene. "I'd want to fight if I knew I did nothing wrong!"

"She told me as a Christian she had to. It wasn't quick, and it wasn't just one time. Some days she'd wake in a bad mood and take it all back, thinking it was too unfair."

"What do you mean 'it wasn't just one time'?" asked Sophie.

Gene was certainly able to identify with Mr. Phillips's client. He felt what was happening to his father was way too unfair.

"Have you all ever heard the old Indian proverb about the wolf?" Mr. Phillips asked.

"No," answered Gene.

He looked at everyone else. They shook their heads.

"A young Indian asked his grandfather how he was so at peace after being injured by another member of their tribe. 'Well,' the grandfather replied, 'it's like I have a bad wolf on one shoulder that tells me to get even and a good wolf on the other shoulder, telling me to forgive. They fight each other.' 'Who wins?' asked the grandson. 'The one I feed' was the answer."

Gene liked that explanation because it created a visual picture. He realized he still fed the bad wolf, but he pictured himself listening to the good wolf. It made him feel a tiny bit of relief.

Maybe I can forgive—eventually.

"I don't know if I can go that far," said Sylvia. "Forgiving these people is hard enough, but I never want to see another courtroom after this is over . . . ever!"

"One thing I've learned is no one is ever prepared for cross-examination. That's why I questioned you the way I did beforehand," said Mr. Phillips.

"I'm sure all one needs to do is tell the truth," Darwin said. "The truth will prevail."

"That's what most people think. However, being on the witness stand is worse than even normal public speaking. Everything rides not only on what you say, but also on how you say it. Prosecutors are trained to take advantage of your nerves," added Mr. Phillips.

Gene asked, "Will we be able to get a fair trial?"

He sank into a chair and folded his arms across his chest. He had a sinking feeling if things did not go right for Mr. Phillips's other client despite her prayers, his prayers might go unanswered too. He knew he had not exactly been listening much to God as a result of the constant anger inside him.

"Unfortunately, our system is filled with men who are sinful beings and don't always do the job they're paid to do. Whether it's misguided, careless interpretation of the facts or outright maliciousness, the end result: innocent people get hurt and the system gets a black eye."

"So is this why you suspect the prosecutor may resort to trickery or outright deceit? Is this the same prosecutor you and the client you spoke about dealt with?" asked Sylvia.

She took a sip of her coffee. From the look on her face, Gene wondered if her faith felt tested also.

Maybe she has been praying for an instant victory with all kinds of bitterness in her heart, just like me.

"Yes, unfortunately, it is. I believe he'll cheat when he thinks it'll get him a victory. Winning: that's all that counts to some prosecutors. That's how they move up the career ladder. It's not about seeking the truth. It's our system's dirty little secret."

"So are you also saying you refuse to play dirty, even if your opponent does?" asked Sylvia.

"Yes. I am. I know I risk losing, and it bothers me a lot more than I'm showing. However, I believe I have to do the right thing no matter how much it hurts, no matter what the cost!"

"I thought you had to fight fire with fire," Gene blurted out.

"I confess I agree with Gene," Sylvia revealed. "I'm not sure I want an honest lawyer if I'm going against a dishonest prosecutor. I can't believe I just said that, but it's honestly how I feel at this moment."

"I know, but that's why I want to help prepare all of you—especially you, Charles—for testifying. I also know how to trap this guy and go for a win on appeal. However, I don't like surprises; I want to be ready for tomorrow. Maybe we can even hope for a mistrial. In that case, we can motion to get Ted out of jail.

"Your first lawyer could have also, if he had submitted the proper requests. I still can't believe they let that guy continue to practice law when he makes such simple mistakes!"

"Then can't we sue him?" asked Gene. "I just want to sue someone!"

"Yes, we can, but it would do you no good. He most likely doesn't even carry malpractice insurance and has probably already spent the money you gave him."

John Phillips looked at Sylvia's coffee.

He added, "I think I want some more coffee after all, if you still have some."

"Sure," answered Sylvia. "Sophie, will you mind getting Mr. Phillips a cup of coffee?"

"No problem, but I can't understand why grownups like coffee so much."

Sophie made a face to show her feelings about coffee. Mr. Phillips noticed and chuckled.

He continued, "I don't like this aspect of the law. I know from experience, reporting him to the bar association will have no results. For some reason, the judges tolerate him."

"I guess I'll consider that an answer to prayer. I mean, getting Ted home again. It kills me to see such a decent husband and father locked up for no just reason! I think with all I've had to adjust to, just having him back with us will be enough to keep me going with whatever else happens," said Sylvia.

A tear trickled down her cheek.

"I'm still trying to cope with the idea that the system will cheat before admitting they got the wrong guy. It makes me wonder how many other innocent men, or women, there might be behind bars. I've always agreed with those who said, 'Lock 'em up and throw away the key!' or 'Everyone says they're innocent . . . they just don't want to take responsibility for their crimes.'"

"So how do you think the system should be changed?" asked Sophie. She handed Mr. Phillips his coffee and a container of French vanilla creamer.

"It'll take a long time to answer that, but I think officers of the law should abide by the same commitment as doctors: first, do no harm. Judges should follow a restorative, rather than punitive model of justice. Police should be put on notice that bullying isn't tolerated and they won't be fired when they honestly try to protect someone. Then they won't feel a need to file criminal charges after every encounter."

Gene asked, "What do you mean by 'restorative' justice?"

He looked at the adults' coffee and wanted to get himself something hot to drink. Yet he did not want to miss any of the discussion.

"In our present system, we ask three questions: What law was broken? Who did it? What's the punishment? With restorative justice, you ask: Who was harmed? Who was responsible? How can it be restored . . . made right? If we applied *that* to your case, Gene, you'd not be charged with anything, and while your dad would still have been a person of interest, he wouldn't be in jail now.

"I think we need trained jurors as well. There really is a lot that jurors need to know in order to discern the truth and reliability of the evidence. For one thing, the fact is that eyewitness testimony as evidence isn't as strong as you might first think. Studies have been conducted to prove just how unreliable eyewitness accounts can be when details are purposely or inadvertently supplied.

"Another thing, all jurors should read at least a summary of the book that explains these studies. One book I read gives examples of people convicted of a crime, later proven innocent through DNA. Over five hundred individuals have been exonerated, some having spent twenty years or more in prison . . . a couple even on death row."

"Wow!" said Gene and Sophie together.

"You already sound as if you've been thinking this issue through," said Sylvia. "I think I'm ready to sign your petition."

"You know what?" asked Gene. "I think I'm beginning to see how similar investigating the facts of a court case is to investigating the facts of a scientific theory. It's all about starting with the prejudices, or wrong ways of looking at things. It's all about, what's the word? Pre . . ."

"Presuppositions," said Mr. Phillips.

CHAPTER 41
DAMIEN'S DEMISE

WEDNESDAY, JUNE 10
12:20 AM

Damien lay in the bed and tried to open his eyes, but they did not open. Nor did his hands move, not even his fingers. He thought he must be dreaming.

It's probably time for my alarm clock to ring. I'm wide enough awake to be aware but unable to move, he assured himself.

However, he heard several muffled voices.

I can't be at home. Where am I?

Thinking made his head hurt. He felt like he was experiencing a migraine. Then mercifully, he drifted off to sleep again.

When Damien came out of the fog of sleep again, he had no idea how much time had passed. However, his thinking was a little more lucid. He perceived he must be in a hospital.

They're talking medical-ese. Something about blood loss . . . potential organ failure. It sounds as if they're saying they need to decide soon if someone will come to or is braindead. The person next to me must be in a coma. Maybe they'll talk about me.

He wanted to know how he got there. He did not remember anything. He tried to remember something, anything. He wanted to fall asleep, but he was unable. It was too boring to stay awake, and he began to feel a painful headache at the back of his head.

⚗ ⚗ ⚗

Marsha arrived at the hospital a lot later than she anticipated. She knew her boyfriend was in serious condition, but she did not realize how serious until she talked to the nurse at the front desk.

I really need to get those reports done. I can spend a couple hours at the hospital and not feel guilty. I hope it won't be too long; I hate hospitals.

She got directions from the nurse and walked down a corridor, turned left, and headed toward the third door on the right.

No! Why can't they make hospitals that don't wind and twist so much? He must be to the left. Yes!

There he was, sound asleep and looking peaceful. He did not look too bad, other than the gauze bandage wrapped around his head.

Marsha walked in Damien's room quietly. She whispered his name: no response. She tried squeezing his hand: no response. She watched him sleep and felt sorry for him. She was not sure if she felt sorry he was in a coma. She had been contemplating breaking up with him, but she could not do that under the circumstances.

She did not like all the feelings of guilt that assaulted her.

Guilt is a toxic emotion and a waste of time—you make your decisions and go with the results. Guilt gets in the way of being decisive.

She had been so into her thoughts, she did not hear the doctor enter Damien's room. When he began to speak, she jumped.

"Sorry to scare you, ma'am," said the handsome forty-something doctor.

He had alert blue eyes and graying, well-groomed hair.

"I'm Damien's doctor. Are you next of kin?"

"I'm Damien's girlfriend. We live together," she said.

Marsha almost wished she had not owned up to being Damien's girlfriend.

This doctor is so cute!

She also noticed he wore no wedding ring on his left hand.

"Has anyone explained Damien's situation to you yet?"

"Just that he's still in serious condition."

"Actually, he's in critical condition. He has gone into shock from blood loss. He hit his head pretty hard when he fell. We assume the two incidents have each contributed to his deep coma. We have him hooked up to monitors and have noticed some heart murmurs, but frighteningly little brain activity. Do you know of any other conditions he has: heart problems, diabetes, or other health problems?"

"Damien has been pretty healthy most of the time I've been with him, but he does have a tendency toward hypoglycemia, or low blood sugar," Marsha replied. "He's supposed to get his blood checked about every six months, but he hates going to the doctor. So I don't know how long it's been since his last checkup."

"Who is his family doctor?"

"Sheesh, I don't know. He never mentioned it."

"Well, this does help a little. We're waiting for the lab reports to come back. Does he have any other family nearby?"

"No. Damien's parents died in a car accident when he was sixteen. He was an only child. I don't know about anyone else. He didn't like to talk much about his family."

"Well, at this point, I can't promise a happy outcome. Comas are tricky to predict. I hate to be so blunt, but does he have a will?"

"Uh, yes, but he's not that bad off, is he?"

"At this point, we'll wait and see. It may become necessary to decide whether or not to revive him should he get worse—he isn't breathing on his own at the moment. I noticed he marked he wanted to be an organ donor on his driver's license. We may need someone to consult with about that issue should he not show any signs of brain activity. "

"So you're saying he has no brain activity?"

"No. He does have some, but it's sporadic; not very much."

"Then you don't think he'll come out of his coma?"

"We don't know. He can wake up today, or in ten years."

Marsha turned to look at the pathetic figure she referred to as her boyfriend. She heard the doctor's hard leather soles pound down the hospital's sterile corridor.

Ten years?

Marsha was having trouble taking all of it in. She suddenly felt his loss. The previous day, she had considered dumping him. Yet she felt a horrible loss.

What if he just holds on like this for years?

She was unable to deal with his potential state of limbo. She wished Damien would either get better or die. She prided herself on being so decisive. 'Go for the gusto, and live with the consequences' was her self-proclaimed motto, but she found herself filled with so many foreign and unwelcome emotions.

"You wished I showed more emotion, Damien," she found herself thinking out loud. "If you only knew how many emotions I'm experiencing right now! Well, you got your wish.

"Oh, Damien, are you still in there! The doctor just gave me a pretty grim forecast. It was easy to talk about our do-not-resuscitate wishes to give our dead corpses to science when I thought it would be far into the future before I had to deal with it.

"Oh, look at me now. I've gone all weepy. A body is just a bunch of chemical reactions. Why am I letting those chemical reactions get to me?"

Marsha shuddered. Not at Damien's predicament, but at hers.

Ten years! No way. Why wait that long when science can benefit sooner? Why wait that long when I can benefit?

"If it comes to a decision, I'll carry out your wishes, Damien, dear. I'll pull the plug."

"Where's that doctor?" Marsha wondered aloud.

She did not dare utter aloud the rest of her thoughts. After having vented all her emotions, she found them drying up at the thought of ten years of him in a coma.

No! I can't, I won't endure that.

Damien drifted back to consciousness.

Something about that voice is familiar. It's a sweet, comforting female voice, but it sounds distressed. Something's wrong. Why is that voice so upset?

He found himself fading away again.

Wait. Have to stay conscious. Who is that speaking . . . Mom? No, she's dead. I'm not dead if I'm thinking.

As the voice continued, it suddenly dawned on Damien it was Marsha, his girlfriend. She had come, although they had been so distant lately. He had begun to worry she no longer loved or cared for him.

She must care!

The thought comforted him until her words began to clear in his mind: "Damien, I'll pull the plug."

Pull the plug? What plug?

Then his foggy mind finally comprehended. He was on life support and Marsha was going to pull the plug to end his life.

No!

He wanted to scream. He wanted to move—anything to show her he was still alive. He did not want to die.

I'm too young . . . I have too much yet to do! It's not fair! God, no . . . God, please!

Damien believed God did not hear him. He felt God had never heard him before. Not when he begged God to save his mother and father after the crash. Not when the bullies at the boys' school he attended mercilessly teased him. Not when his first crush rejected him.

No. There's no God.

He did not believe it. He wanted to get out of the hospital, finish his research, and prove there was no God. Then he might even marry the only person who had ever been kind to and appreciated him—Marsha.

Unfortunately, no matter how hard he struggled, nothing moved. He was unable to utter a sound. He felt trapped within his body, and the fog was coming in again. He tried to fight it, but it overtook him. Damien drifted back to sleep for the last time as Marsha pulled the plug.

CHAPTER 42
WIN, LOSE, OR DRAW

9:00 AM

Gene grew tired of being in the courtroom. It was pretty with a lot of fancy woodwork, but its décor did not make it a nicer place to wait when waiting to find out how the rest of one's life was going to go.

If Dad's found guilty, what'll happen? Will we be able to survive? Will he even be able to enjoy Christmas at home?

With all the commotion of his father's trial, Gene kept forgetting he also faced charges if his father was convicted. He wished his friends were there so he had someone to distract him from all his worries. He wished he had a cell phone like other kids his age had. Instead, he had to use an old-fashioned land line, but there were none available in the waiting area.

He wondered what his friends were doing. C. M. had become strangely quiet. He had not talked with him since the night he and Sophie had met Darwin. Actually, he had not talked to Kaleb either. Suddenly, Gene felt tremendous zing of anxiety.

Alexis!

He covered his agonized expression with his hands and slunk as low as possible on the hardwood bench. He had been so consumed by the events of the trial, he had completely forgotten about his promise to try yet again to meet Kaleb and Alexis at the mall the previous day. He had made the arrangement over a week ago.

Has that much time really passed?

He was shocked to realize he had not thought much about her the past few days. Two weeks ago, she was all he thought about.

What am I going to do now?

Finally, Mr. Phillips came out of Judge Goode's chambers. He waved for Sylvia, Gene, and Sophie to follow him as he headed toward one of the private rooms nearby. When they were all present, he closed the door and smiled.

"Well, we haven't won, but the next best thing happened."

"You were in there for so long," Sylvia said. "What happened?"

"The prosecutor tried to pull a fast one and change the charges. According to him, the charges needed to be updated since Damien Agnossi passed away."

"He did?" asked Gene and Sophie at the same time.

They looked at each other in astonishment. It was news to everyone.

"Oh my," Sylvia said with a sigh.

Her breathing began to reveal her fear—she appeared ready to hyperventilate.

"I'm sorry. I thought you all knew. It was on the news last night. However, don't worry. This actually helps Ted," Mr. Phillips said.

"I mean, I'm saddened by this news, and it does have the possibility of worse problems, but for now, the prosecutor actually gave us a break by changing the charges. Since this case has taken so long to come to trial, changing the charges at this point allows us to request a new trial. That's precisely what I intend on doing. Since we had the extra day, I also came prepared with a couple versions of a motion to request bail. The judge hinted he'll grant the new trial and he's open to a bail hearing."

"So does this mean Ted will get out of jail today?" Sylvia asked with hope.

"No, not today, but we'll get the bail hearing in a day or two. Since I now have more information and evidence, I may be able to challenge the validity of the arrest and Ted's detention and request a ruling on whether or not his rights were violated.

"Right now, however, we need to be back in court in ten minutes. It shouldn't take long," Mr. Phillips explained. "Then if the judge does give us a new trial, you all may go home as soon as we get the date for the next hearing. I'll need to talk to Ted, but I want you to know, even though I must always caution my clients not to get too excited, I feel good about what's going to happen in the next few days!"

"So this nightmare will soon be over?" asked Sylvia.

"Not over, but it should start taking a turn in our favor."

"I'll settle for hopeful," said Sylvia.

Gene was afraid to let himself hope for the best. He was afraid it might jinx everything.

CHAPTER 43
BETRAYED

As it turned out, Mr. Phillips had been right. They got their new trial and the bail hearing was set for the next day. A pretrial hearing was also set for the end of the next week. Then court was dismissed.

Gene was able to breathe. They were not able to talk with Ted, but the smile he had exchanged with them before the guards took him back to his cell was encouraging.

It seemed to take Sylvia forever to finish talking to Mr. Phillips. Finally, she came outside and unlocked the car for Gene, Sophie, and Darwin. They got inside the car and headed home. As Gene listened to his mother talk, he thought things sounded good for his father, yet his anxiety level was high. He was unable to quit shaking his foot. Dealing with the trial and all its complications was nerve-wracking.

How can I be so forgetful? A date with Alexis and I totally flaked . . . I'm such a nerd. I keep messing up. I wonder why Kaleb hasn't called. He's probably mad at me too.

He wanted to call Kaleb as soon as possible. Before the car even came to a complete stop in their driveway, Gene opened the door.

"Gene, wait until I stop the car!" shouted his mother. "What's the hurry?"

"He's got to make a phone call," teased Sophie.

Gene ignored her remark. He got to the telephone in the den and shut the door. He called Kaleb. The call went to voicemail. Gene left an urgent message.

"Kaleb, I've been so busy with this court stuff, I forgot to call to let you know I couldn't make it to the mall. Did you go? Did you see Alexis? What did she say? Call me as soon as you can."

He let out a sigh and started to leave the room, then turned and grabbed the telephone again. After seven rings, C. M. answered the telephone.

"Yeah?"

"Hey, C. M., I've been so busy I forgot to meet Kaleb and Alexis at the mall yesterday. Have you talked to Kaleb lately?"

"What? No. Uh . . . Hello . . . How are you?"

"Oh, sorry, I've been so hyped all morning waiting to hear what's going on with my dad and trying to get to a phone. So how are you? Hey, what ever happened that night at the lab?" Gene asked. "Sheesh, that's how messed up my head's been. Why'd you ditch us? We had to hitch a ride in an Amish buggy."

"Long story, but I basically got busted. I tried to hide from the security guard and ran right into the cops. So, I got picked up for curfew violation; my mom and stepdad are making me spend the summer with an aunt in Pennsylvania. I'd rather have had your problem," C. M. explained. "An Amish buggy? Now that's too funny."

"It wasn't at the time. Dude, I'm sorry. I didn't know you got in so much trouble. I thought you ditched us."

"No. I'd of at least called you the next day and laughed at you."

"So I guess you haven't talked to Kaleb, have you?"

"No, but I heard some rumors. Are you sitting down?"

"I am now. What's going on?"

"Well, I don't know how to tell ya, but rumor is Alexis is going with Kaleb now."

"What!"

"Sorry, dude. It happens. Yeah, you really need to call Kaleb. It might not be true. You know how rumors get started."

Gene was so upset he slammed the telephone down.

"That double-crossing . . ."

He punched the sofa cushion and fell onto it. He covered his face with his hands.

"It figures. Why can't I just have one good day!"

CHAPTER 44
LOOSE ENDS

Gene took time to absorb everything that was happening. He felt an urge to call Kaleb and confront him. He hoped the rumor was not true, and he needed to talk to a friend. He picked up the telephone and noticed he had four unanswered calls from Kaleb.

"Shoot!" Gene hissed. "I can't believe I forgot to meet Kaleb. Not twice, but three times!"

I should probably give Kaleb the benefit of the doubt before I accuse him of anything. Maybe C. M. heard wrong. I hope he heard wrong.

So he pushed the speed-dial button for his best friend since kindergarten.

"Hey, so did you talk to Alexis? Does she like me? I meant to call you back days ago, but I've been busy with all that's going on with my dad."

Gene was so excited he did not notice how quiet his friend was. Kaleb was normally quite a bit more talkative.

He continued, "You won't believe what I discovered at my dad's lab! You gotta get over here so I can tell you all about what's been going on."

"Uh, Gene, I think I should interrupt you here and give you some bad news."

"What's that?" asked Gene.

He finally slowed down.

This is gonna be bad news.

Gene prayed his friend was okay and the rumor was false.

"Um, I don't know how to say this to you, but just straight out. Are you ready for some bad news?"

"Did someone die?" asked Gene in a serious tone.

"No, but you may want to kill someone after I tell you."

"What? Just spit it out!" Gene was beginning to get annoyed.

"Alexis has a boyfriend now."

"What . . . how? I mean . . . who?"

"Um, that's the hard part."

"Who is it? Just tell me!"

Kaleb confessed, "It's me." The line got silent.

"Say again," said Gene.

"It's me."

"You're kidding me, aren't you? Don't mess with me like that!"

"I'm not kidding."

"But . . . you never said anything about liking her. You knew I was crazy about her. How could you?"

Gene stood up started to pace as he held the telephone, and tried not to get tangled in the cord.

"It just happened, dude!"

"What do you mean, 'It just happened' I thought you were trying to help me!"

"I did, Gene. I did talk to her about you. She had nice things to say about you, but when you didn't meet us after school and I walked her home . . . well, we just got to talking, and we kept on talking after we got to her house.

"Then I called her later because I forgot to tell her where to meet us the next day. We talked for two hours! I've never talked to a girl that long. I wasn't trying to hit on her, I swear! We just hit it off.

"Then the same thing happened the next day when you failed to show up again. One thing led to another and she told me she was more interested in me," Kaleb explained. "It shocked me. I've not had a girlfriend or any girl like me since first grade! She came on to me!

"Sorry, man, but what can I say? I didn't want to hurt her feelings. Then I realized I wanted her for myself. How bad can you want her if you kept avoiding us?"

"I wasn't avoiding you. I had stuff to do. Stuff I was all set to tell you about, but you know what? Not now. I don't want to tell you about that or anything else. I don't even want to talk to you ever again!"

With that, Gene slammed the telephone down.

CHAPTER 45
VINDICATED

THURSDAY, JUNE 11

Gene's head was swimming. Mr. Phillips had warned them Prosecutor Mangil might try something, and he had. Gene was stunned. He looked over at his mother and sister, who were still in shock but stoically tried to keep their emotions in check. However, none of them were able to speak yet. It was as if they held their breath for fear of bad news.

Maybe it's better Mr. Darwin isn't in here to hear this.

Darwin was in the waiting area with Noah in case he was called to testify once more. Gene seriously doubted Prosecutor Mangil wanted to do that again.

Mr. Phillips had lived up to his reputation of being a tough advocate. At first, he had held his temper and Gene was impressed. He had thought if it had been him, he might have exploded on the prosecutor and judge. It was so obvious the prosecutor was being malicious and vindictive; the judge seemed to allow it. It was all Gene could do to keep himself from yelling out how stupid and unfair the whole trial was.

After only ten minutes, the arguing in the courtroom had escalated to the point that Judge Goode warned Mr. Phillips and Prosecutor Mangil they risked contempt charges if they did not stop arguing. Then he had called them into his chambers, which had been forty-three minutes ago.

Gene looked at his watch again.

Forty-four minutes now.

Time was going so slowly. He did not want to think about the previous night's conversations with his friends.

How am I gonna make it through the summer?

His best friends were out of the picture, and his father might also be gone. Gene was tired of waiting and wanted to know what was happening.

What's the verdict? What's going to happen to Dad?

He had been watching Ted while Mr. Phillips and Prosecutor Mangil had been arguing. Gene was unable to tell what his father was thinking. How he wished for a chance to know. He even thought about how he wanted to have family nights every night if that persuaded God to let his father go free.

His thoughts spurred another line of thinking. Gene knew he was going to make it up to his father for all the mean things he had said about those family meetings: they ruined his life; he was too old for such baby stuff; and he had a personal life, or rather, wanted to have a personal life and go out with his friends.

Gene was not doing bad stuff like some of the kids he knew at school. He just wanted some independence.

While he had been thinking about how badly he had treated his father at their last family meeting, Ted had turned and caught his gaze. It was just a moment, but their eyes met. Ted smiled and winked: a sign to Gene that he believed everything was going to work out, and that he loved him. Then Ted faced forward.

It amazed Gene how much that momentary glance had communicated. It made him realize how lucky he had been to have a father who had cared enough to make his family a priority. None of his other friends did. As a matter of fact, C. M. did not even have a caring father. His stepdad, or whatever he called him, was not even married to C. M.'s mother.

From what C. M. had said of his real father, he did not sound much better. No wonder his friend had started changing. Yeah, it kind of hurt that C. M. had not returned his calls, but he knew C. M. was going through a rough time. That was what really hurt—his friend had not even told him the truth about what was going on with him.

No, it hurt worse to see C. M. hang out with some of his rougher classmates, some of whom he had heard were deep into the drug scene; especially when C. M. had brushed Gene off about a planned outing like their last game night. That fateful night before everything had gotten out of whack.

Back when I still had friends.

Gene remembered his last conversation with Kaleb.

That double-crossing dog . . . His mom sure had named right!

He knew from his Bible classes that Kaleb, or Caleb from the Old Testament, meant "dog."

How could Kaleb take my girl?

It did not matter that Alexis was not officially his girl. However, Kaleb knew how head-over-heels Gene was about her. He had been since she first walked into his science class at the beginning of the semester. It had taken him months to work up the courage to talk to her about hanging out with him. He shook his head.

His life had really gone downhill in such a short time. He had thought life was rough before their legal fiasco. He knew now he had had it good. He had wanted to be treated as a grownup, but he realized he just wanted to be a kid.

Growing up sucks!

If this was what it felt like to be an adult, Gene wanted none of it. It was too painful.

He started to think of Alexis again but stopped himself. It made him feel like such a failure. He'd messed up every chance to get to know Alexis; now she was with his ex-best friend. His science teacher had rejected his report for being one day too late. He was glad he'd answered that call and not his mom.

He'd wrestled so long with what to write for his report, and it was all for nothing now. Too bad he couldn't have just brought Darwin into his class for show-and-tell. He'd have gotten an "A."

Then remembering Darwin, Gene quietly got up to go check on his friend. Darwin looked worse than Gene felt.

So Gene sat down next to his new friend and whispered, "Hey, Mr. Darwin, you don't look too good. Are you feeling okay?"

"Thanks for thinking of me, Gene. I feel a little queasy, but otherwise okay."

"Okay. I just don't want to see you hurl all over the floor again. Give me some warning if you feel that way so I can move!"

"Hmph. Yes, I will," Darwin replied with sadness.

"Why are you so sad? Are you missing your family?"

"Thanks for asking, but no. I'm actually thinking of your family. I feel somewhat responsible for your father's problems . . . on several levels."

"You? You're not responsible for anything. You're the key witness!"

"Actually, I'm the key reason your father is even here today. I feel just horrible about it! If I hadn't tried to help that man the way I did, or perhaps if I hadn't hidden in the closet, there might not even be a need to have this trial!"

"But that's not your fault. You can't help having been dragged from your time into the lab! You were just trying to help. I don't blame you for being confused. If those bozo detectives woulda investigated things like they were supposed to and waited until they had all the facts, we wouldn't be here either."

"Yes, once again, trying to help, I had that accident all over the prosecutor," Darwin said. "That's why we're in this courthouse, isn't it?"

"I hardly think you can be blamed for getting sick. At least you finally found out why you have stomach problems and got some good meds for it."

"Yes. I suppose that's good. I'm very grateful to your mother for getting me such wonderful medical treatment. The advances in medicine since my father practiced medicine are quite marvelous and astounding!" Darwin said. "On another note, even the whole issue of evolution, the theory I proposed and published, is at the heart of the reason we're here."

"How so?"

"Think about it. If your father and this Damien character weren't trying to test my theory, they never would've done the experiment. There would've been no accidental time machine, and I never would've been brought forward in time to be there to harm Damien and cause so many problems for your father!"

"Hmm. I never thought of it that way."

Gene had not and found the thought gave him an odd feeling. He felt he was supposed to be upset by the revelation, yet another part of him wanted to comfort his friend. Then the thought struck him as odd.

The *Charles Darwin is my friend.*

"Oh, don't blame yourself for that!" Sophie said, interrupting Gene's thoughts. She and his mom had just come out the courtroom door. Sophie always seemed to say what he wanted to say to make others feel at ease.

She continued, "I believe God has a reason for your being here, and even for all we're going through. I don't begin to claim to know why, but I believe we'll soon find out."

Gene asked, "Do you think Dad will get out of jail today?"

"I don't know, but last night while you guys were sleeping, Mom and I prayed. Neither of us was able to sleep, so we prayed first for God to help us accept whatever happened today and still have faith He'll answer our prayer to free Dad. I don't usually pray that way; I usually beg God to give me what I want. However, after Mr. Phillips told us he suspected something might go amiss today—and after he told us about the other lady and how she saw a lot in hindsight that she was unable to see at the time—I really felt at peace after we prayed, and so did Mom."

"Why didn't you ask me to join you?" asked Gene.

"Actually, we did try. Mom tapped on your door, but after several knocks and no response, she said we should just let you sleep if you were able to sleep," Sophie answered.

"Actually, Gene, I'm sort of surprised you're bothered by missing our prayer group," interrupted Sylvia. "We would've been glad to have you join us."

EPILOGUE

There they were. It had been so long since he had been free to touch those he loved. Ted grabbed all of them—Sophie, Gene, and Sylvia— and gave them the biggest bear hug he had ever given in his life.

"Dad!" yelled Sophie. "You're squishing me!"

"Oh, sorry," said Ted.

He tried to hold back tears to say something else, but the dam broke. The tears fell unapologetically.

"It's okay," replied Sophie as she teared up. "It's just soooo nice to have you back."

"I was afraid this day would never come," added Sylvia. She alternately sobbed and laughed with joy.

"Yeah, ditto," said Gene. He tried to hold back tears, despite all the crying going on around him. He succeeded until he saw his dad's red eyes.

It was not too long ago when he would have preferred to be dead than show anyone, especially his father, any public affection. However, he was doing just that . . . crying. He wondered if it meant he was maturing or simply acting like a baby. At that point, it did not matter who saw him—he was glad to have his father back. Gene wanted to say more to welcome Ted back, but he was afraid his voice might betray more emotions.

Instead, he just observed the bearded individual he knew as Dad, but who looked so very different. His clothes hung loose on him too. Ted seemed to have changed in other ways as well. Gene was unable to put his finger on it, but something definitely had changed about his father.

"Well, as glad as I am to see you all, can we get out of this place and go get some real food—pizza or steak?"

"Pizza!" shouted Gene and Sophie.

Gene turned to go and saw Darwin standing to the side. He had a smile on his face but seemed sad as well.

"Oh, Dad," called Gene, "there's someone we want you to meet. This here is Charles Darwin—*the* Charles Darwin!"

Ted looked at Darwin incredulously and then raised his hand to shake Darwin's hand.

"I hear you helped me get my freedom back," said Ted.

"Actually, sir, I'm afraid I'm the cause of your troubles. If I had never been in that lab or tried to help that man and then ran, you never would've had to incur such discomforts and trouble."

"Well, let's just say you've made my life interesting," said Ted with a crooked smile.

"And you have made my life interesting. You were the architect of that machine, were you not?"

"Yes, I put that machine together, but I don't think you caused my problems. It was the way the detective, police, and that prosecutor handled everything. If they had actually investigated the crime scene instead of jumping to conclusions, all my legal problems would never have been.

"But let's not talk about that now. I'm more concerned about getting some real food and then discovering how my time machine worked to bring you forward in time. That just boggles my mind. I can make a lot of money off a time machine. That is, if anyone believes you're who you are."

"Oh, believe me," said Gene, "he's who he says he is. You shoulda seen the first time he saw an automatic door. He jumped ten feet!"

"Tell Dad how many times he had to flush the toilet," added Sophie.

"Yes, but at least I do know what pizza is. Now, that my stomach problems have almost gone away I do believe I'd like a meat lover's supreme," replied Darwin with a laugh.

"Oh, yes, that sounds great!" Ted agreed as they exited the courthouse.

△ △ △

They sat at a table with three empty pizza boxes, save crusts, and talked about the future.

"It's been great to catch up on all that's happened since I was thrown in jail," Ted said. "You have no idea how much I missed you . . . and good food!"

"So what are you going to do now? I mean, do you still have your job?" asked Gene.

"Well, I've had a lot of time to think about that. I want to finish any commitments I still have there, but I really want to accept that offer by the Institute for Creation Research," answered Ted. "I'd love to do research for creation instead of evolution. No offense, Charles, but I really believe the evidence for creation is right under our noses if we will but acknowledge it."

"No offense taken," said Darwin. "Honestly, I've been confronted with so many new facts; I need to re-evaluate my theory. Now, wouldn't that be ironic if I joined you in disproving my theory!"

Everyone laughed. Then Darwin moved a pizza box and folded his hands on the table.

"I've been thinking. Since I can't go back in time—and believe me, I have no desire to experience time travel again, no matter how much I may miss those I left behind—I'd love to study at one of your universities and learn more about all the glorious discoveries made in science since my time."

Sylvia said, "I can help you with that. I was about to say how much I wanted everything back to normal, but I no longer know what normal is! I've learned to trust God more through this experience. Mr. Phillips is taking care of everything now, so I think I can wait on God to take care of the rest of the court issues. After seeing how He took care of things at trial . . . well, that was quite the surprise ending!"

"Yeah, it brought up the worst in some of us," said Gene as he looked at Darwin.

"Oh, you can say that again," Darwin agreed with a laugh. "So, my young friend, you never did tell me what conclusions you came to about my theory."

"I'll let you read my report when I finish it. I had to rewrite it. I had to give my teacher my first draft, but I want to revise it before I let anyone else read it"

"I have something for you to read too."

Darwin slid his hand into his jacket and pulled out a diary.

"I think you'll enjoy this, my good friend. I can't tell you how helpful you and your sister have been in helping me adapt to my new surroundings."

Gene took the book and looked at it. It was Darwin's diary. He was barely able to wait to read it. Before he opened it, his sister stood and grabbed for it.

"No way; I get to read it first."

Sophie dropped back to her seat with an angry sigh but missed it and landed on the floor. She started to laugh but noticed everyone staring at her.

"I'm okay, really."

Then she noticed what everyone was staring at. The fall had caused her pant leg to hike up enough to expose a red spot.

"Uh-oh."

"Sophia Lynn Kysen, what have you done?" asked her mother with disapproval.

"Oops! Ahh . . . yes, there's a wee little issue I forgot to tell you guys about with all the other stuff going on. On a dare, I got this tattoo.

It wasn't supposed to be a real one, but . . . well, it was. It cost more money than I had," she explained.

"Since I'd borrowed Dad's sweater and it had his credit card . . . well, long story short, I used it. I've got the money to pay you back in my bank account!"

"That was you?" Ted asked and rubbed his face. "I thought that was Gene. I never had a chance to talk to him about it. We'll most definitely talk more about this later, young lady."

"So that's what that 'little thing' was that you wanted to talk to me about? I got in trouble for something little Miss Goody Two-Shoes did?" Gene glared at his sister.

"Oh, Gene," Ted said as he closed his eyes and rubbed his face. "I owe you a big apology. I had a lot of time to think about how hard I'd been on you, taking my job stress out on you. I'm really sorry, son. Will you forgive me?"

Gene was speechless. He was shocked at what his sister had had the nerve to do, and even more at his father's sincere apology. Maybe under normal circumstances he might have held a grudge against his father, but he had time to do a lot of thinking as well.

"Of course," he said when he realized his dad was still waiting for an answer.

"Thanks, Gene. I heard all these legal proceedings messed up your final grades. What about your science report? How are you handling all this?"

"Well, it really bugged me that my science teacher didn't accept my report late, especially after I put all that work into it. I don't think I deserved to fail. I wish teachers were not allowed to fail us. Fortunately, Mom came to my rescue and got my teachers to have mercy on me. I don't know when she had time to call them, but she did.

"My science teacher said he'll give me an incomplete until I hand in a 'proper' report. That way, I don't have to retake science class. The other teachers worked with me. Besides, I found the report a lot easier to do since I dealt with my confusion about so many of the issues between evolution and creation. Did you know both theories claim DNA as evidence? Since DNA was an important factor in your trial, I thought about it a lot. Do you know what I discovered?"

"What?" asked Ted.

"When you take the letters for the chemicals that make up DNA, G, C, A, and T, they can also stand for 'God Created All Things'!

"I actually like solving the mysteries of science. I think maybe I want to become a research scientist like you, Dad. Or maybe become a forensic scientist and solve crimes!"

"Me too!" added Sophie. "That'll be so cool to help solve crimes. Or else, I want to become a paleontologist and study fossils of dinosaurs and dragons . . . and just date boys who like science. Who knows, maybe I'll find the missing link—"

"Missing link!" exclaimed Gene. "I didn't think you, of all people, believed in evolution."

"No, not *that* missing link . . . If you'd let me finish! I want to find a link between man and dinosaurs living at the same time, like fossil footprints or bones of both in the same place."

"Oh, maybe you can prove dragons and dinosaurs are the same thing," Gene teased.

"That's my next project," replied Sophie and then stuck out her tongue at her brother. "Don't be so quick to make fun of the idea. There really is a lot of proof. Come on, I'll show you this new book I have."

"After I read this," Gene said as he held up Darwin's diary.

For more information about
LINDA MCBRIDE
&
NOT ALLOWED TO FAIL
please contact:

Grandmalinda5.3@gmail.com

....

For more information about
AMBASSADOR INTERNATIONAL
please visit:

www.ambassador-international.com
@AmbassadorIntl
www.facebook.com/AmbassadorIntl